Realm of Enchantment Tales from the Mystic Lands

Morgan B. Blake

Published by CopyPeople.com, 2024.

Table of Contents

The Curse of Eldergrove 1
The Shadows Within 4
The Heart of the Thief 8
Flames of Unity 11
The Moonlit Grove 15
The Unraveled Spell 19
The Siren's Search 23
The Guardians of Eldoria 27
The Heart of a Prince 31
The Whisper of the Wild 35
The Bookshop of Wonders 39
The Blade of Destiny 43
The Sorcerers of Seasons 47
The Heart's Divide 50
The Whispering Oak 54
The Petals of Elyndra 58
Beneath the Shadows 62
The Orphan's Crown 66
The Doorway in the Meadow 70
The Heart of the Guardian 74
The Island of Lost Dreams 78
Reflections of Desire 82
The Wishkeeper 86
The Canvas of Dreams 90
Whispers of the Forgotten 94
The Arcane Brotherhood 98
The Elemental Trials 102
The Healer of Aeloria 106
The Shadow of Aeloria 110
The Eternal Flame 114
The Guardian's Oath 117

The Alchemist's Legacy	121
The Land of Giants	125
The Garden of Wishes	128
The Star-Crossed Maiden	131
Wings of Fire	135
The Awakening of Thalassa	139
Beneath the Surface	143
The Dragon's Choice	147
The Storm of Transcendence	151
The Chosen Flame	155
The Elixir of Ambrosia	158
The Dreamweaver's Realm	161
The Curse of the Jewel	165
The Valley of Enchantment	169
The Secrets of Sylvan Grove	172
Threads of Destiny	175
The Warding of Willow Creek	179
The Gilded Shadows	183
The Guardian of Aetheria	187
Get Another Book Free	191

Created by the CopyPeople.com[1]
All rights reserved.
Copyright © 2005 onwards .
By reading this book, you agree to the below Terms and Conditions.
CopyPeople.com[2] retains all rights to these products.

The characters, locations, and events depicted in this book are fictitious. Any resemblance to actual persons, living or dead, events, or locations is purely coincidental. This work is a product of the author's imagination and is intended solely for entertainment purposes.

All rights reserved. No part of this book may be reproduced, stored in a retrieval system, or transmitted in any form or by any means—electronic, mechanical, photocopying, recording, or otherwise—without the prior written permission of the publisher and the author, except in the case of brief quotations embodied in critical articles and reviews.

The views and opinions expressed in this book are those of the characters and do not necessarily reflect the official policy or position of the author, publisher, or any other entity. The author and publisher disclaim any liability for any physical, emotional, or psychological consequences that may result from reading this work.

By purchasing and reading this book, you acknowledge that you have read, understood, and agreed to this disclaimer.

- Thank you for your understanding and support.
- **Get A Free Book At:** https://free.copypeople.com

---

1. https://copypeople.com/
2. https://copypeople.com/
3. https://free.copypeople.com

The Curse of Eldergrove

In the heart of the Eldergrove Forest, a village named Bramblewood thrived under the watchful gaze of its ancient trees. Among its residents was Lyra, a young mage whose affinity for nature's magic was unmatched. With fiery red hair and emerald green eyes, she was often found dancing with the wind or coaxing flowers to bloom. However, beneath the beauty of her surroundings lay a dark secret—an ancient curse that had long threatened the village.

The curse originated centuries ago when a powerful sorceress named Seraphina, jealous of the villagers' happiness, cast a spell that would bring despair upon them every harvest moon. For years, the village had remained untouched, but as the next harvest moon approached, an ominous shadow loomed over Bramblewood. Crops began to wither, the river's water turned murky, and an eerie silence enveloped the forest. The elders of the village gathered, their faces lined with worry.

"Lyra," Elder Marwen called, his voice trembling. "You possess the gift of magic. We need your help to lift this curse before it consumes us all."

Lyra's heart raced. She had studied the ancient texts, but facing a curse was different from reading about it. "What must I do?" she asked, her determination surging through her veins.

"The source of the curse lies within the Grove of Whispers," Marwen explained, gesturing toward the thickest part of the forest. "There, you must confront the spirit of Seraphina. Only by facing her can the curse be lifted."

As the sun dipped below the horizon, Lyra set out toward the Grove of Whispers. The forest seemed alive, shadows flickering between the trees. She could feel the weight of the curse pressing down on her, and with each step, she whispered incantations to bolster her courage. When she reached the grove, an otherworldly chill wrapped around her like a cloak.

"Who dares disturb my slumber?" a voice echoed, cold and melodic. The air shimmered, and before her materialized the spirit of Seraphina—beautiful yet terrifying, with eyes like storm clouds.

"I am Lyra of Bramblewood," she declared, her voice steady despite her fear. "I am here to break the curse you placed upon my village."

Seraphina's laughter echoed through the grove, a sound that chilled Lyra to her core. "You think a mere child can undo my work? This curse is my gift to remind them of the darkness that exists within."

Lyra clenched her fists, drawing on the magic within her. "Darkness may exist, but so does light. You have let your bitterness blind you to the beauty of life. Your curse has only brought pain."

The spirit's eyes narrowed, intrigued by Lyra's conviction. "And what will you offer me to lift this curse?"

"I will share my magic with you," Lyra proposed, "to show you the joy you once knew. You have the power to change."

Seraphina paused, a flicker of vulnerability crossing her face. "Magic cannot erase the past, child."

"Perhaps not, but it can help you create a new future," Lyra replied softly, her heart full of empathy. "Join me, and together we can restore the balance you once cherished."

The spirit hesitated, and for a moment, the forest seemed to hold its breath. "Very well," she said, her voice softer now. "Show me this magic of yours."

Lyra extended her hands, and vibrant flowers bloomed at her feet, their colors bright against the darkened grove. She conjured a gentle breeze that danced through the trees, whispering tales of laughter and love. The spirit watched, enraptured, as Lyra wove the magic of the village into the air.

For the first time in centuries, a smile broke across Seraphina's ethereal face. "Perhaps I have forgotten the beauty of this world."

As Lyra continued to share her magic, she felt a change in the atmosphere. The curse began to lift, the shadows receding as light flooded the grove. But just as she thought victory was at hand, the ground trembled violently. A surge of energy erupted, and Seraphina began to dissipate.

"No!" Lyra cried, reaching out to her. "What's happening?"

"I cannot remain in this world," the spirit said, her voice echoing as if from a great distance. "But know this—by breaking the curse, you have freed me from my own prison of despair. My power will no longer haunt Bramblewood, but it will not vanish completely. It will become part of you."

With that, Seraphina vanished into a cascade of shimmering light, leaving behind a sense of profound peace.

Returning to Bramblewood, Lyra was greeted with cheers. The crops had regained their vitality, and laughter filled the air once more. The villagers embraced her, but Lyra felt a bittersweet pang in her heart. She had saved her home but at the cost of losing Seraphina.

In the weeks that followed, Lyra discovered that the spirit's magic flowed within her, granting her deeper powers and understanding. She learned that true strength lay not only in wielding magic but in facing darkness with compassion.

As the next harvest moon approached, she stood in the center of the village, now a beacon of hope. Lyra smiled, knowing that the lessons of Seraphina would guide her forever. The greatest magic, she realized, was not the ability to banish darkness but to embrace it and transform it into light.

The Shadows Within

In the hidden realm of Eldoria, where magic thrived like wildflowers and ancient secrets whispered through the wind, an ambitious sorcerer's apprentice named Kaelin sought to carve his name into the annals of history. His master, the venerable Sorceress Elara, was a beacon of wisdom, renowned for her mastery over the arcane arts. Kaelin, with his fiery red hair and restless spirit, yearned for greatness, but he often found himself fumbling through spells and misreading ancient tomes.

One fateful evening, while sifting through dusty scrolls in the grand library of Eldoria, Kaelin stumbled upon a foreboding manuscript—the Codex of Shadows. Its pages were filled with dark incantations and prophecies about an ancient evil named Malakar, a sorcerer whose insatiable hunger for power had led to his banishment centuries ago. The manuscript warned that Malakar was poised to rise again, unleashing chaos upon the world unless someone intervened.

Kaelin's heart raced as he read the words. "The day of reckoning approaches. The apprentice must confront the darkness within to thwart the resurrection of Malakar." A chill crept up his spine. Was it truly his destiny to stop such a malevolent force?

Determined to prove his worth, Kaelin sought Elara's counsel. "Master, I've found a dire prophecy. Malakar will return, and I must prepare to face him!"

Elara, her silver hair shimmering in the candlelight, regarded him with a mix of concern and pride. "You've stumbled upon a great truth, Kaelin. But be warned, confronting Malakar requires more than just power. You must be willing to confront the darkness within yourself."

"I will do whatever it takes," he vowed, his resolve burning bright.

The next day, Kaelin embarked on a journey to gather the tools necessary for his quest. He traversed enchanted forests and perilous mountains, facing mythical beasts and treacherous traps. Along the way, he forged alliances with beings of light: a mischievous fairy named Lirael, who wielded illusion magic, and Thorne, a stoic guardian of the ancient runes, whose strength was unmatched.

Together, they sought the three sacred artifacts capable of sealing Malakar's essence: the Amulet of Purity, the Chalice of Harmony, and the Mirror of Truth. Each artifact lay hidden in locations steeped in myth and guarded by trials that tested their resolve.

Upon reaching the Temple of Purity, Kaelin faced a harrowing challenge. The temple's guardian, a fierce phoenix, demanded a sacrifice—a piece of Kaelin's heart, representing his fear and doubt. Trembling, he hesitated, but Lirael's encouraging words echoed in his mind. "True strength comes from embracing your fears, not hiding from them."

With a deep breath, Kaelin offered his fear to the phoenix. The moment he did, a brilliant light enveloped him, and the Amulet of Purity emerged, shining with a warmth that dispelled his doubts.

The next trial took them to the Cavern of Echoes, where they sought the Chalice of Harmony. Here, they encountered a monstrous shadow, a manifestation of Kaelin's inner turmoil. It whispered cruel taunts, dredging up every mistake he had ever made. "You're not worthy, apprentice! You'll never be a true sorcerer!"

Fury ignited within him, but instead of fighting back, Kaelin faced the shadow. "I am not defined by my mistakes. I am more than my failures!" He summoned the Amulet, channeling its light into the shadow. The darkness shrieked, dissipating into shimmering dust, leaving behind the Chalice of Harmony.

With two artifacts secured, the trio set their sights on the final challenge: the Mirror of Truth, hidden deep within the Crystal Glade. Upon arriving, they were greeted by the mirror's crystalline surface, reflecting not only their images but their innermost fears and insecurities. Kaelin stared at his reflection, seeing a version of himself consumed by darkness, a failed sorcerer lost in despair.

But then he remembered the trials he had faced and the friends he had made along the way. "I am not alone," he declared. "I am stronger than my fears. I will not succumb to darkness!"

In that moment, the mirror shattered, revealing the Mirror of Truth, a gleaming shard of crystal that pulsed with energy. With all three artifacts in hand, Kaelin and his friends returned to the ancient site of Malakar's imprisonment.

As they began the ritual to seal Malakar away, the ground trembled, and a swirling darkness erupted around them. Malakar's spirit manifested, a shadowy figure draped in malevolence, his laughter echoing through the air. "Foolish children! You think you can stop me?"

Kaelin stood firm, drawing upon the power of the artifacts. "You may have been powerful once, but you are not stronger than the bonds we share and the light we carry!"

In a climactic battle, Kaelin unleashed the combined magic of the amulet, chalice, and mirror, engulfing Malakar in a blinding light. The dark sorcerer roared in fury as he was drawn back into the abyss, the artifacts sealing his essence once more.

As silence fell over the land, Kaelin's heart swelled with pride. They had triumphed, but as the dust settled, he felt a shift within himself. The real battle had not just been against Malakar, but against the darkness inside him—the doubts, fears, and insecurities he had harbored for so long.

Lirael and Thorne approached him, their expressions filled with admiration. "You did it, Kaelin!" Lirael exclaimed.

"I couldn't have done it without you both," Kaelin replied, a newfound humility washing over him. "I've learned that true strength lies not in power alone, but in friendship, acceptance, and facing one's own darkness."

And so, as the sun rose over Eldoria, Kaelin stood not just as a sorcerer's apprentice but as a true sorcerer—a beacon of hope for all, forever changed by the shadows he had faced and the light he had embraced.

The Heart of the Thief

In the bustling city of Eldenmere, where the sun barely penetrated the smoky haze of the marketplace, a thief named Rylan navigated the crowded streets with a deftness born from years of practice. With tousled dark hair, a sly grin, and nimble fingers, he was a ghost among shadows, slipping in and out of stalls, snatching small trinkets and purses with ease. His reputation as the city's most notorious pickpocket was well-earned, but Rylan craved more than mere survival; he longed for a life of luxury and adventure.

One fateful evening, as the moon cast a silvery glow over the cobbled streets, Rylan's instincts led him to a decrepit antique shop hidden between two larger buildings. The shop's sign creaked ominously, its lettering faded and barely legible. Intrigued, he slipped inside, his eyes darting around the dimly lit room filled with dusty relics and forgotten treasures.

As he explored, Rylan's fingers grazed over various objects, each with its own history, until he came across a wooden chest intricately carved with swirling patterns. Heart racing with excitement, he opened it, revealing a dazzling gemstone pulsating with an otherworldly light. It was the fabled Heart of Aetheria, an artifact rumored to grant its wielder immense power and influence over fate itself.

"Take it," a voice whispered from the shadows, startling him. An elderly woman with a haggard appearance emerged from behind a curtain. "But know this: such power comes with a price."

Ignoring her warning, Rylan pocketed the gemstone, his greed blinding him to the potential consequences. "I'll take my chances," he smirked, leaving the shop and stepping into the night, the heart's glow illuminating his path.

Over the next few days, Rylan discovered the artifact's astonishing abilities. With a mere thought, he could manipulate luck—turning near captures into escapes, transforming meager finds into bountiful treasures. His notoriety grew, and soon he was known not just as a thief but as a master of fate. Wealth and power flowed into his hands, and he reveled in his newfound status.

But with great power came great temptation. Rylan began to indulge in excess, throwing extravagant parties and flaunting his riches. Friends became sycophants, drawn to his fortune rather than his character. The thrill of stealing turned into a game of one-upmanship, with Rylan always seeking more—more wealth, more power, more influence.

Yet as the days passed, the Heart of Aetheria began to reveal its darker side. Rylan noticed that his manipulations were not without repercussions. Each time he twisted fate, someone else suffered. A merchant he swindled lost his livelihood; a rival thief fell victim to misfortune and ended up in prison. The city he once loved now felt foreign, its people mere pawns in his game.

One night, as he sat alone in his lavish chamber, the weight of his choices crashed over him like a tidal wave. He could see the faces of those he had wronged, their eyes filled with despair. The Heart pulsed ominously, as if mocking his internal struggle. Rylan's heart ached, and he realized that his quest for power had cost him his soul.

In a moment of clarity, he made a decision. Rylan would return the Heart of Aetheria to the antique shop and undo the chaos he had caused. It was time to face the consequences of his actions and restore balance to his life.

Under the cover of darkness, he made his way back to the shop. The old woman was waiting for him, her eyes glinting with an unreadable expression. "You've come to return it," she stated matter-of-factly.

"Yes," Rylan admitted, his voice steady but filled with remorse. "I can't keep this. It's corrupted me."

With a knowing nod, she took the Heart from him. "You've learned the lesson that many never do: power without responsibility breeds destruction. You've taken much, but you can also give back."

"What do you mean?" Rylan asked, confused.

The woman smiled gently. "You have the choice to mend what's been broken, to use your skills for good. There is still time to change your destiny."

Rylan felt a spark of hope ignite within him. "How?"

"Begin with the people you've wronged," she replied. "Use your talents to help them rather than harm them. The true heart of a thief lies not in what he takes, but in what he gives back."

Inspired, Rylan spent the following weeks making amends. He returned stolen goods, helped struggling merchants, and used his cunning to expose corrupt officials. As he rebuilt his relationships, he felt lighter, the darkness of the Heart lifting with each act of kindness.

In time, Eldenmere transformed as Rylan transformed. The city flourished, filled with laughter and camaraderie, and he found a new purpose among its people. No longer a mere thief, Rylan became a protector of the downtrodden, a champion for those in need.

The Heart of Aetheria, once a symbol of greed, became a reminder of the lesson learned: that true power lies in humility, responsibility, and the choices we make in the shadows of our lives. And in the end, Rylan discovered that destiny is not a fixed path but a tapestry woven from the threads of our actions, forever changing with each choice we make.

Flames of Unity

In the kingdom of Eldoria, where majestic mountains pierced the sky and lush valleys sprawled beneath them, a bitter rivalry existed between dragons and knights. For centuries, these two forces had clashed, driven by misunderstandings and ancient grudges. But fate had a way of weaving its own tapestry, and a common enemy was about to emerge that would challenge the very foundations of this rivalry.

Sir Cedric, a valiant knight known for his unparalleled swordsmanship, stood at the edge of the Great Forest, his heart heavy with the weight of his duty. News had spread of a dark sorcerer, Malakar, who sought to awaken an ancient evil buried beneath the mountains. If Malakar succeeded, all of Eldoria would fall into chaos. The knights of the realm had sworn to protect the kingdom, but Cedric knew that alone, they stood little chance against the sorcerer's dark magic.

As he ventured deeper into the forest, the wind whispered warnings, and shadows danced among the trees. Suddenly, a thunderous roar erupted from above, causing the very ground to tremble. Cedric looked up just in time to see a massive dragon, its scales shimmering like emeralds in the sunlight, descending toward him. He instinctively reached for his sword, ready to fight, but something in the dragon's eyes—intelligent and wary—stopped him.

"Do not draw your weapon, knight," the dragon spoke, its voice a deep rumble that resonated in Cedric's chest. "I am Zephyr, and I have no quarrel with you... at least, not today."

Cedric hesitated, lowering his sword slightly. "Why are you here, dragon?"

"The sorcerer Malakar seeks to unleash a darkness that will consume all, even dragons," Zephyr replied. "I can sense the corruption spreading through the land. We must put aside our differences and join forces if we are to stop him."

Cedric's mind raced. The idea of allying with a dragon was unthinkable, yet the urgency of the situation weighed heavily on him. "Very well," he said, gripping the hilt of his sword with resolve. "But know that I will not hesitate to defend myself if you betray me."

With a nod, Zephyr spread his enormous wings, lifting Cedric off the ground and soaring toward the mountains. Together, they traversed the skies, the knight clinging tightly to the dragon's neck, feeling a thrill of adventure mixed with fear.

As they reached the craggy peaks, they spotted Malakar's fortress—a dark tower shrouded in swirling clouds. The air crackled with ominous energy, and the ground pulsed beneath them. "We must be cautious," Zephyr warned. "The sorcerer is powerful, and he has summoned creatures to guard his lair."

With a shared glance of determination, they descended, landing quietly at the base of the fortress. As they approached, they encountered twisted creatures of shadow—malformed beings that hissed and clawed at the air. Cedric unsheathed his sword, and Zephyr unleashed a torrent of fire, incinerating the first wave of attackers.

Together, they fought valiantly, the knight's swordsmanship complementing the dragon's fiery breath. As they battled, Cedric began to see the dragon not as a fearsome beast, but as a noble ally, fighting for a shared cause. Zephyr, in turn, recognized Cedric's bravery and honor, qualities that transcended the knight's human nature.

After what felt like hours, they finally reached the door of the tower. With a heavy thud, Cedric kicked it open, revealing Malakar seated on a throne of obsidian, his dark robes flowing around him like a shadow. He looked at them, amusement flickering in his eyes.

"So, the knight and the dragon come to challenge me," Malakar sneered. "How quaint."

"Your reign of darkness ends here, sorcerer!" Cedric declared, his voice echoing off the stone walls.

Malakar rose, raising a hand, and the air shimmered with dark energy. "You are fools to think you can defeat me! I have the power of the ancient evil at my command!"

In a moment of desperation, Cedric looked at Zephyr. "We need to combine our powers!" he shouted.

Zephyr nodded, understanding the unspoken plan. As Cedric charged forward, he concentrated his energy, and with a mighty roar, the dragon unleashed a colossal fireball that intertwined with Cedric's sword, amplifying its light.

The two forces collided with Malakar's dark magic, creating a brilliant explosion of energy that lit up the chamber. The sorcerer screamed as the combined might of knight and dragon overwhelmed him, shattering his dark aura and banishing him into oblivion.

As the dust settled, Cedric and Zephyr stood victorious, breathing heavily. "We did it!" Cedric exclaimed, his heart swelling with triumph.

But as the remnants of Malakar's magic faded, a strange light emanated from the center of the room. A portal opened, revealing a swirling vortex. "What is that?" Cedric asked, wary of the unknown.

"It is the essence of the ancient evil," Zephyr explained. "We must seal it away, or it will find a way to return."

Realizing that sealing the portal would require a sacrifice of their combined power, Cedric looked at his newfound ally. "Are you willing to do this?"

Without hesitation, Zephyr replied, "Yes, for the sake of our future and this kingdom."

They joined hands, channeling their remaining strength into a binding spell. As they cast it, the portal closed with a blinding flash, leaving behind a sense of calm in the air.

In that moment, Cedric felt a shift within himself, a deeper understanding of unity and sacrifice. The rivalry between dragons and knights had blinded them for far too long. As the dust settled, he looked at Zephyr, their bond stronger than any history of enmity.

"Together, we are stronger," Cedric said, realization dawning on him.

Zephyr nodded, his eyes gleaming with newfound respect. "And together, we can rebuild the trust between our kinds."

As they emerged from the fortress, they found the sky clearing, the sun breaking through the clouds. Cedric knew that the path ahead would not be easy, but with allies forged in fire and trust, they could face any challenge together.

In the end, the lesson was clear: unity in diversity could overcome even the deepest divides, and from the ashes of rivalry, a new alliance had been born—one that would protect Eldoria for generations to come.

The Moonlit Grove

In the quaint village of Eldergrove, tales of an enchanted forest hidden beneath the full moon danced on the lips of old wives and children alike. The elders spoke of the Moonlit Grove, a magical place that emerged only when the moon hung full and bright in the night sky. It was said that within its depths lay treasures beyond imagination and secrets that could alter destinies. Yet, it was equally whispered that those who entered seeking fortune might never return.

Lila, a curious and adventurous soul, had heard the stories since childhood. With chestnut hair and a spirit that craved exploration, she often dreamt of the grove, captivated by the legends that filled her mind with wonder. As the next full moon approached, she felt an undeniable pull towards the mythical forest, an itch in her feet that begged to be scratched.

On the night of the full moon, Lila donned a simple cloak and set out into the night. The village lay silent, the air thick with anticipation as the moon bathed the world in silver light. She followed a winding path that led her beyond the familiar, her heart racing with excitement and trepidation.

As she ventured deeper into the woods, the trees began to shimmer, their leaves glistening like starlight. Suddenly, the air shifted, and the forest around her transformed. Lila stepped into the Moonlit Grove, where ethereal flowers bloomed, and wisps of light danced in the air. The vibrant colors of the foliage contrasted sharply with the darkened night, creating an otherworldly beauty that took her breath away.

"Welcome, seeker," a melodic voice echoed through the grove. Lila turned to see a figure emerging from the shadows—a woman with long, flowing hair adorned with luminous blossoms. Her skin glowed faintly, and her eyes sparkled with ancient wisdom.

"Who are you?" Lila asked, captivated yet cautious.

"I am Selene, guardian of the Moonlit Grove," the woman replied, her voice like a gentle breeze. "You have come seeking something. What is it that you desire?"

Lila hesitated, the weight of her desires pressing down on her. "I wish to find my purpose. I feel lost, adrift in a world that doesn't understand me."

Selene regarded her with a knowing smile. "Many come seeking fortune or power, but true treasure lies in self-discovery. If you seek your purpose, you must prove yourself worthy."

Lila's heart raced. "How?"

"Follow the path of the silver stones," Selene instructed, gesturing to a trail that shimmered beneath her feet. "You will encounter trials that reveal your true self. Overcome them, and your purpose will be unveiled."

With a nod, Lila stepped onto the path, determination igniting her spirit. The first challenge awaited her—a towering wall of vines that seemed to whisper her fears. They taunted her with words of doubt, echoing the insecurities that had plagued her for years.

"Turn back, Lila. You are not strong enough," the vines hissed.

But with a deep breath, she recalled the stories of brave heroes and the strength that lay within. "I am more than my doubts!" she shouted, pushing through the vines with all her might. To her surprise, they parted effortlessly, revealing the next challenge.

Before her stood a shimmering lake, its surface still and clear. As she approached, images began to appear in the water—visions of her childhood, moments of joy, and times of sorrow. The reflection began to distort, showing her failures and the disappointments that haunted her.

"See what you are?" the water whispered. "You are defined by your mistakes."

"No!" Lila declared, clenching her fists. "I am shaped by my experiences, not bound by them." With that declaration, the lake shimmered and transformed into a mirror, reflecting her true self—a brave, determined woman ready to embrace her journey.

Continuing along the path, she faced one final trial: a bridge made of moonlight suspended over a chasm of darkness. It wobbled and swayed, the void below filled with shadows that seemed to reach for her.

"Step onto the bridge, Lila," Selene's voice echoed from somewhere beyond. "Trust in your own light."

With her heart pounding, Lila stepped onto the shimmering bridge. It felt fragile beneath her feet, but she focused on the light within her. Each step illuminated her path, dispelling the shadows. She reached the center, where the light grew brightest, and in that moment, she understood.

"I am my own purpose," she whispered, realization washing over her like a tide. "I have the power to shape my destiny."

As she stepped off the bridge, the grove erupted in a cascade of light, illuminating the night sky. Selene appeared before her, radiant and proud. "You have faced your fears and embraced your truth. Your purpose lies not in grand deeds but in the courage to be yourself."

"Thank you," Lila said, tears of gratitude welling in her eyes. "I feel... free."

"Remember, the Moonlit Grove exists to remind you of the light within. It will return when the moon is full again, but your journey continues beyond these woods." Selene smiled, and the grove began to fade, the vibrant colors softening into the shadows.

Suddenly, Lila found herself back in the familiar woods outside her village, the moon shining brightly above. The grove had vanished, but the lessons remained etched in her heart.

As she walked home, a newfound sense of purpose filled her. She understood that the journey of self-discovery was ongoing, and it was up to her to embrace it. The enchanted forest may have disappeared until the next full moon, but the magic of her awakening would stay with her forever, guiding her through the trials of life.

In the end, Lila learned that true purpose is not a destination to be found but a light to be nurtured within—a lesson that would illuminate her path long after the moon had set.

The Unraveled Spell

In the quaint village of Eldermere, tucked away between rolling hills and dense forests, magic thrummed in the air. It was a place where the mundane and the mystical intertwined, and where the rumors of witches and spells danced through the whispers of the townsfolk. At the heart of this enchanted world lived Isolde, an eager apprentice under the tutelage of the village's most revered witch, Morwenna.

Morwenna was a powerful sorceress, known for her mastery of charms and hexes, but she was also notorious for her strictness. "Patience and precision are the keys to magic," she often reminded Isolde, her piercing blue eyes locking onto the apprentice's. "One slip, and you could unleash something beyond your control."

Isolde was determined to prove herself worthy, but her impatience often got the better of her. On a particularly stormy night, while Morwenna was away gathering rare herbs, Isolde found herself alone in the cottage, surrounded by an array of dusty tomes and bubbling cauldrons. One book caught her eye—a thick, leather-bound volume with intricate designs etched on its cover. It was the *Grimoire of the Abyss*, rumored to contain spells both forbidden and powerful.

Ignoring the creeping sense of caution, Isolde opened the grimoire, her curiosity piqued. Pages filled with incantations and sigils dazzled her. Her fingers danced over the text until they landed on a particularly enticing spell—one that promised to summon a spirit of immense power. "What could go wrong?" she mused, a mischievous grin spreading across her face.

Gathering the necessary ingredients—an owl feather, a pinch of salt, and a drop of her own blood—Isolde began the ritual. She spoke the incantation with a confident flourish, her voice resonating in the dimly lit room. As the final words escaped her lips, the air crackled with energy, and the room swirled with an unnatural wind.

Suddenly, the ground beneath her trembled, and a blinding flash filled the space. When the light receded, Isolde stood frozen in shock, staring at the massive figure that materialized before her. It was a demon, towering and imposing, its skin a shimmering red, with eyes that burned like embers.

"Foolish girl!" the demon roared, its voice echoing like thunder. "You have summoned me, and now I am bound to your will!"

Isolde's heart raced as she scrambled backward. "I-I didn't mean to! I just wanted to prove I could do magic!" Panic surged through her as she realized the gravity of her mistake.

The demon, unfazed by her distress, leaned closer, an amused glint in its fiery eyes. "You think you can control me? I am Tzothar, an ancient being of chaos. Your feeble magic means nothing to me!"

"Wait!" Isolde exclaimed, her mind racing. "If you're bound to my will, then maybe I can—"

"Bound?" Tzothar laughed, a sound that sent chills down her spine. "You cannot bind me; you merely called me forth. And now, I will wreak havoc upon this village unless you find a way to send me back."

Isolde felt the weight of dread settle on her shoulders. She needed to think fast. "What if we made a deal? If you spare my village, I'll help you return to your realm."

Tzothar raised an eyebrow, intrigued. "A deal? You think you can bargain with a demon?"

"Yes!" Isolde said, grasping at straws. "I can find a way to break your curse if you help me learn real magic in return. Imagine the power you could wield if you teach me!"

The demon regarded her for a moment, then smiled—a grin that revealed razor-sharp teeth. "Very well, apprentice. I will grant you one lesson in exchange for your village's safety. But know this: the price of magic is often higher than anticipated."

Before she could respond, Tzothar raised a hand, and the room shimmered with energy. Suddenly, Isolde found herself in a different realm—an expanse of swirling shadows and flickering flames. Tzothar stood beside her, his presence commanding.

"Welcome to the Shadowlands," he announced. "Here, I will teach you the true nature of magic."

As Tzothar demonstrated his powers, conjuring storms of fire and manipulating shadows, Isolde's awe began to shift into fear. The magic he wielded was intoxicating but chaotic, and she soon found it difficult to differentiate between creation and destruction.

"Power without control is dangerous!" Isolde shouted as Tzothar unleashed a torrent of flames, threatening to engulf her. "I don't want to hurt anyone!"

"Then embrace the chaos!" Tzothar replied, his voice booming. "You cannot harness true magic without understanding its wild nature."

In that moment, Isolde realized that her desire for power had blinded her to the responsibility that came with it. "No!" she declared, shaking her head. "I don't want to be like you!"

Fueled by newfound determination, Isolde focused on the essence of her own magic—her connection to the natural world and the protective spells Morwenna had taught her. Drawing upon that energy, she conjured a barrier of light that pushed back against Tzothar's flames.

"You think you can resist me?" the demon roared, but Isolde stood firm, channeling her will.

With every ounce of strength, she forced Tzothar back, the shadows retreating from her light. "I will not be your puppet! I will send you back where you belong!"

In a blinding flash, the Shadowlands collapsed around them, and Isolde found herself back in her cottage. Tzothar shrieked as the light enveloped him, his form disintegrating into shimmering embers.

"No! You will pay for this insolence!" he howled before vanishing completely, leaving Isolde breathless.

As silence fell over the cottage, Isolde slumped to the floor, her heart pounding. She had faced her fears and discovered the true nature of magic—not as a tool for power, but as a responsibility to wield wisely.

When Morwenna returned, Isolde recounted her harrowing experience. The witch listened intently, a mixture of pride and concern in her eyes. "You have learned a valuable lesson, my dear," she said softly. "Magic is not merely about strength. It is about understanding yourself and the world around you."

From that day forward, Isolde embraced her path as a witch, focusing on the harmony between power and responsibility. She would never forget the demon she had summoned, nor the chaos that ensued. In her heart, she understood that true magic was not about control but about balance—a lesson that would guide her as she continued to learn and grow.

The Siren's Search

In the vibrant depths of the Coral Kingdom, where the sunlight pierced the water in shimmering rays, lived a mermaid named Lirael. With flowing sea-green hair and iridescent scales that glimmered like gemstones, she was a guardian of the ocean's beauty. Yet, her heart ached with sorrow, for her beloved sister, Seraphine, had vanished one moonlit night. Despite the merfolk's tales of human sailors taking mermaids captive, Lirael knew in her heart that Seraphine had ventured above the waves for a reason.

Determined to find her sister, Lirael made a bold decision. She would leave the safety of the ocean and navigate the treacherous waters of human society. Under the glow of the full moon, she transformed her tail into legs with a spell learned from an ancient sea witch, her heart racing with both fear and excitement as she stepped onto the shore.

The sandy beach felt foreign beneath her feet, the salty breeze brushing against her skin as she took her first tentative steps. Lirael watched the bustling human world around her—people gathered in lively groups, laughter mingling with music from nearby taverns. Though she had studied humans from a distance, the vibrant energy was overwhelming.

As she wandered through the coastal town, Lirael marveled at the lights and colors of human life. Her wide eyes caught the attention of a local fisherman, a rugged man named Dorian, who noticed her hesitation. "You look lost, miss," he said, his voice warm and inviting. "First time in the village?"

Lirael hesitated but decided to trust him. "I'm searching for someone—my sister. She may have come to this shore."

Dorian's brow furrowed with concern. "Many travelers come and go. Tell me what she looks like, and I'll help you find her."

With every detail, Lirael described Seraphine, her laughter like the tinkling of shells, her beauty radiant as the sun. Dorian nodded, determination in his eyes. "I'll ask around. In the meantime, you should stay close. Humans can be unpredictable."

Days turned into weeks as Lirael immersed herself in human life, learning their ways while continuing the search for Seraphine. Dorian became her closest ally, guiding her through the complexities of the human world. They explored the market, tasted fruits she had never seen before, and shared stories beneath the stars. In the warmth of their growing friendship, Lirael began to feel a sense of belonging.

One evening, as they walked along the shore, Lirael spotted a beautiful shell glimmering in the sand. As she bent down to pick it up, a rush of memories flooded back—images of Seraphine collecting shells during their childhood. Clutching the shell tightly, a sudden thought struck her. "What if my sister has been captured by one of the sailors?"

Dorian's expression turned serious. "There are stories of mermaids being taken aboard ships. We must be cautious, Lirael. It's dangerous."

Determined, Lirael decided to infiltrate a local tavern where sailors often gathered. She needed information, and the best place to hear stories was where the men shared their adventures. Dorian, though worried for her safety, agreed to accompany her, insisting on looking out for her.

Inside the dimly lit tavern, laughter and music filled the air, mixed with the scent of salt and ale. Lirael took a deep breath, the tension rising in her chest as she approached a group of rough-looking sailors. Dorian stood nearby, ready to intervene if things escalated.

"Excuse me," Lirael began, her voice steady but soft. "I'm looking for my sister. She's a mermaid—have any of you seen her?"

The sailors paused, their laughter fading. One of them, a burly man with a scar across his cheek, leaned closer. "Mermaids, eh? You sure you're not just chasing tales, lass?"

"I know she's real," Lirael replied, meeting his gaze. "And I will find her."

The atmosphere shifted, and the sailors exchanged glances. Finally, the scarred man chuckled, a low, rumbling sound. "I might know a thing or two. But what's in it for me?"

Dorian stepped forward, ready to defend her. "You'll tell us what you know, or I'll make sure you regret it."

Before the situation could escalate, Lirael raised her hand, calming the tension. "Please, I just need to know where she is."

"Fine," the man said, leaning back in his chair. "A ship passed through here a few nights ago. They had a captive—a mermaid, no less. Took her with them, said they were heading north to the kingdom of Thalassia."

Lirael's heart raced with a mix of hope and fear. "Do you know the name of the ship?"

"The *Sea Serpent*," he replied, his voice now laced with a hint of respect for her determination. "But it won't be easy to get to her."

Dorian placed a reassuring hand on Lirael's shoulder. "We'll find a way. You have the heart of a true warrior."

With the information in hand, Lirael felt a surge of resolve. The next morning, she and Dorian set out to find the *Sea Serpent*, racing against time. They traveled along the coast, questioning fishermen and sailors until they finally located the ship anchored in a harbor.

As night fell, Lirael and Dorian devised a plan. Lirael would use her mermaid form to slip aboard the ship while Dorian kept watch from the shore. She transformed beneath the waves, her tail shimmering in the moonlight as she glided toward the ship.

Once aboard, Lirael searched desperately for Seraphine, navigating the ship's darkened corridors. Finally, she heard a familiar voice—her sister's laughter, echoing through the cabin. With a mix of joy and urgency, she pushed open the door, only to find Seraphine in a room surrounded by the ship's crew, engaged in a lively celebration.

"Seraphine!" Lirael gasped, relief flooding her. But as she stepped inside, her sister turned, her eyes wide with surprise.

"Lirael? What are you doing here?"

"I came to rescue you!" Lirael exclaimed, but before she could explain, Seraphine held up a hand, a smile playing on her lips.

"Rescue me? I'm not in danger! These sailors found me lost at sea. They've been treating me like a guest, not a captive."

Confusion washed over Lirael as the crew looked on, puzzled but amused. "You... you're happy here?"

"Yes!" Seraphine replied, her laughter ringing like music. "I've learned so much from them about the human world! It's wonderful."

Lirael felt a pang of disappointment, her heart sinking. "But I came all this way to bring you home."

Seraphine stepped forward, concern in her eyes. "Home is where you make it, Lirael. I've discovered a new path, and I want to explore it. Don't you see? We can both find our destinies in our own ways."

In that moment, Lirael realized the truth: her sister's happiness mattered more than her own fears. "You're right," she said, her voice filled with acceptance. "I can't keep you tied to the past. If this is where you belong, then I will support you."

As they embraced, Lirael felt the weight of her quest lift. She understood that sometimes, love means letting go. With a final wave, she transformed back into her mermaid form, swimming toward the horizon. She would return to the depths of the ocean, carrying the warmth of their bond with her, knowing that they would both thrive in their chosen paths.

In the end, Lirael learned that navigating the waters of life often required more than courage; it required the wisdom to recognize that home is not a place, but a feeling—a lesson that would guide her as she embraced the endless possibilities of the world above and below the waves.

The Guardians of Eldoria

In the heart of the realm of Eldoria, tales of an ancient treasure known as the Celestial Sapphire had spread like wildfire among adventurers and treasure seekers. The gem was said to be hidden deep within the Crystalline Caverns, a labyrinthine network of tunnels guarded by mythical creatures—dragons, griffins, and spirits of the earth. Many had attempted to claim the sapphire, but none had returned.

A group of five adventurers, each with their unique skills and backgrounds, gathered in the bustling tavern of the village of Windhaven. There was Aric, the brooding warrior with a reputation for his unmatched swordsmanship; Selene, a clever rogue with a talent for stealth and deception; Thalia, a fierce ranger whose bond with nature gave her the ability to communicate with animals; and Eldrin, a scholarly wizard with a vast knowledge of ancient lore. Last was Margo, a healer with an unyielding spirit and the ability to mend wounds with a mere touch.

"I've heard the stories," Aric began, his voice low and intense. "The Sapphire is not just a gem; it's said to possess the power to control the elements. If we succeed, we'll be legends."

Selene leaned forward, her eyes gleaming with excitement. "But we must be cautious. The creatures guarding it are not just myths—they are ancient protectors of the realm. We need a plan."

Thalia nodded, a frown on her face. "I can speak to the creatures of the forest. They might provide insight into the dangers we'll face."

Eldrin, thumbing through an old tome, added, "We must also be prepared for traps and illusions. The Caverns are designed to confuse and mislead intruders."

With their plan set, the group embarked on their journey, their spirits high with the thrill of adventure. They traveled for days, facing treacherous terrain and unpredictable weather, until they finally stood before the entrance of the Crystalline Caverns. The air shimmered with magic, and the sound of dripping water echoed ominously from within.

As they entered, the walls sparkled like stars, illuminated by veins of luminous crystals. However, the beauty was deceptive; shadows lurked in every corner, and the air was thick with enchantment.

"Stay close," Aric warned, drawing his sword as they ventured deeper into the caverns.

Suddenly, a low growl reverberated through the tunnels. From the shadows emerged a massive dragon, its scales gleaming like polished emeralds. "Who dares enter my domain?" it roared, smoke curling from its nostrils.

Thalia stepped forward, her voice steady. "We mean no harm. We seek the Celestial Sapphire to protect our realm from impending darkness."

The dragon narrowed its eyes, clearly unimpressed. "Many have claimed noble intentions, yet they all sought only to steal the Sapphire for themselves."

Margo stepped in, her gentle demeanor calming. "We seek to protect, not to conquer. If you let us pass, we promise to honor the treasure and its guardians."

The dragon considered them for a long moment, then gestured with its claw. "Very well. I will allow you to proceed, but you must face the trials of the Caverns. Succeed, and you may claim the Sapphire. Fail, and your souls will remain here for eternity."

With that ominous warning, the dragon disappeared into the shadows, leaving the adventurers to face the first trial. They entered a vast chamber filled with shifting mirrors that reflected their fears. Each adventurer was confronted by an illusion that tested their resolve: Aric faced a vision of himself in chains, powerless; Selene saw her past betrayals laid bare; Thalia was surrounded by withering forests; Eldrin was haunted by the knowledge of his own failures; and Margo witnessed the suffering of those she couldn't save.

Together, they fought against their fears, encouraging one another to push through the illusions. Margo's healing touch provided strength, and Thalia's connection with nature reminded them of their purpose. As they united their wills, the mirrors shattered, revealing a hidden passage leading deeper into the caverns.

The next chamber was guarded by a griffin, majestic and fierce. "Only those who show true bravery may pass," it declared, its golden eyes scrutinizing them. "Prove yourselves!"

Aric stepped forward, ready to fight, but Selene held him back. "We don't need to fight. Let's show our bravery in a different way." She stepped closer to the griffin. "We don't seek to defeat you; we want to work together."

The griffin regarded her with surprise. "Bravery is not always about fighting. Very well, I will allow you to pass, but you must carry my message to the outside world—that peace is stronger than conflict."

With a nod of agreement, the adventurers continued their journey, their spirits buoyed by their progress. Finally, they reached the heart of the Caverns, where the Celestial Sapphire rested on a pedestal of crystal. The sight took their breath away; the sapphire glowed with a soft, inviting light.

As they approached, however, a spirit materialized before them—an ethereal figure with a serene expression. "You have proven your worth, but to claim the Sapphire, you must answer a riddle."

The spirit's voice echoed around them as it spoke:

"I am taken from a mine, and shut up in a wooden case, from which I am never released. What am I?"

The group exchanged glances, the tension rising as they struggled to find the answer. It was Eldrin who broke the silence. "Pencil lead! It's taken from a mine and encased in wood."

The spirit smiled, a warm glow enveloping the chamber. "You are correct. The treasure is yours, but remember: true treasure lies not in the riches you possess but in the bonds you've formed."

As the spirit faded, the sapphire levitated into their hands, its power coursing through them. But instead of taking it for themselves, they shared a glance filled with understanding.

"We need to protect this gem," Margo said, her voice firm. "We can't let it fall into the wrong hands."

Together, they placed the Celestial Sapphire back on the pedestal, understanding that its power was not meant to be wielded by mortals. As they turned to leave, the Caverns trembled, and a hidden passage opened, leading them back to the surface.

As they emerged into the sunlight, the adventurers felt changed. They had sought a treasure but discovered something far more valuable: the strength of their unity and the importance of selflessness.

And so, in the heart of Eldoria, the legendary treasure remained guarded, its power safe from those who would seek it for personal gain, while the adventurers returned home not as legends of fortune but as champions of peace, knowing the true treasure lay in the bonds they had forged along the way.

The Heart of a Prince

In the kingdom of Aetheria, nestled between shimmering mountains and lush valleys, there lived a prince named Alaric. Handsome and noble, he was admired by many. Yet, beneath his charming exterior lay a dark secret: he had been cursed by a vengeful sorceress after spurning her advances. The curse transformed him into a beast by night, a shadow of his former self, while his human form remained intact by day. To break the spell, he needed to win the love of a mortal woman, one who would see past his monstrous facade.

For years, Alaric roamed the vast expanse of his kingdom, seeking companionship yet terrified of revealing his true nature. Villagers spoke in hushed tones of the cursed prince, a figure of both intrigue and horror. He spent his nights in solitude, hidden within the enchanted forests surrounding the castle, wrestling with the duality of his existence.

One fateful evening, as twilight descended and the stars began to twinkle, Alaric stumbled upon a lively village festival. Laughter and music filled the air, beckoning him closer. Caught in the moment, he donned his royal cloak, hoping to blend in with the merriment while remaining inconspicuous. The glow of lanterns illuminated the village square, and Alaric's heart raced as he caught sight of a striking woman dancing amidst the revelers.

Her name was Elara, a spirited healer known for her kindness and wisdom. She moved gracefully, her laughter ringing like a melody that captured his attention. Alaric felt an unfamiliar warmth spread through him. Drawn to her, he approached, determined to learn more.

"Would you care to dance?" he asked, his voice low but inviting.

Elara turned, her deep green eyes meeting his. A smile lit her face. "I would love to, but only if you promise not to step on my toes!" They both chuckled, and together they danced under the moonlight, the music wrapping around them like a spell.

As the evening unfolded, Alaric found himself entranced by Elara's tales of adventure and her dreams of helping others. He felt a flicker of hope—could this be the love that could break his curse? Yet, the shadows of his secret loomed large. Every moment spent with her was tinged with the fear of revealing who he truly was.

As the festival came to an end, Alaric summoned the courage to invite Elara to the castle. "I would like to show you my home," he said, holding his breath. "There's much to see."

Elara's eyes sparkled with curiosity. "I'd be honored. But I hope it's not as gloomy as the tales say!"

The next day, they ventured to the castle. Alaric led her through grand halls adorned with tapestries that told the history of Aetheria. As they walked, laughter flowed easily between them, and Alaric's heart swelled with affection. But the weight of his curse felt heavier as the sun dipped lower in the sky.

As night fell, Alaric's transformation was imminent. He tried to delay it, hoping for a miracle, but as the moon rose high, he felt the familiar tug of the curse taking hold. "Elara," he said, panic rising in his chest, "you should leave. It's not safe for you here."

"What do you mean?" Elara asked, concern etched on her face.

Before he could explain, he was engulfed in a swirl of darkness. When the shadows receded, the beast stood where the prince had been. His fur was dark as midnight, and his eyes glowed with an eerie light.

Elara gasped, stepping back, fear overtaking her. "What have you done? What are you?"

"Please," he growled, though the words were filled with desperation, "I am still Alaric. I was cursed, and I can only break it with love. I never meant for you to see me like this!"

To his surprise, Elara didn't flee. Instead, she took a cautious step forward. "You are still the same person inside, aren't you?"

"Yes," Alaric replied, his voice a low rumble. "But my curse makes me a monster by night. I understand if you wish to leave."

But Elara stood firm, her expression shifting from fear to resolve. "You deserve love just as much as anyone else. I will not abandon you."

For nights, Elara returned to the castle, determined to be by Alaric's side. She learned to see beyond the beast, recognizing the heart that beat within. They shared stories and dreams, laughter and sorrow, and as time passed, the bond between them grew stronger.

One night, after an exhilarating conversation, Elara took Alaric's paw in her hand. "You are not just a beast, Alaric. You are brave, kind, and worthy of love. I want to help you break this curse."

As the moonlight bathed them in silver, Alaric felt something shift within him. "I fear that even if I win your heart, the curse may not be broken. What if I remain like this forever?"

"I will love you no matter what," Elara promised, her voice unwavering. "Your heart is what matters most to me."

As their eyes met, something magical happened. The air crackled with energy, and the light of the moon enveloped them. A blinding flash illuminated the room, and in that instant, the curse shattered. Alaric transformed back into his human form, his features regaining their princely grace.

Tears of joy streamed down Elara's face as she beheld the prince before her. "You did it! You're free!"

Alaric looked into her eyes, overwhelmed with gratitude and love. "No, we did it. It was your belief in me that broke the curse."

However, as the initial excitement faded, Alaric began to realize something profound. The curse had been a test, a way to reveal the true strength of love. "Elara," he said, his voice filled with sincerity, "this experience has shown me that true beauty lies not in appearances but in the bonds we forge through understanding and acceptance."

They embraced, the warmth of their connection radiating through them. From that day forward, Alaric ruled Aetheria with Elara by his side, not just as his queen but as his equal and partner. Together, they taught the kingdom that love transcended appearances and that true strength was found in the courage to embrace one another's flaws.

And so, the legend of the cursed prince became a tale of love, proving that sometimes the heart can conquer even the darkest of curses, forging bonds that last a lifetime.

The Whisper of the Wild

In the quaint village of Elderswood, nestled between lush forests and rolling hills, lived a spirited girl named Lila. With her untamed curls and a heart full of wonder, she spent her days exploring the woods, where the songs of birds and rustle of leaves painted the backdrop of her adventures. She often dreamed of the creatures that roamed the forests, feeling a connection to them that she couldn't quite explain.

One sunny afternoon, as Lila wandered deeper into the woods than ever before, she stumbled upon a hidden glade filled with wildflowers and a crystal-clear pond. Entranced by the beauty surrounding her, she sat down on a mossy rock, taking a moment to appreciate the serenity. Suddenly, she heard a soft voice, like a gentle breeze.

"Why do you sit so far from your home, little one?"

Lila's eyes widened in shock as she turned to find a small fox sitting beside her, its fur glowing in the sunlight. "Did you just... speak to me?" she stammered.

"Of course," the fox replied with a flick of its bushy tail. "You can hear me because you have the gift. Not many humans can understand our words."

Lila's heart raced. "What do you mean? I can understand you?"

"Yes," the fox confirmed, tilting its head curiously. "But it's not just me. You can communicate with all animals. It's a rare talent, and it comes with great responsibility."

Lila felt a mixture of excitement and disbelief. "I can talk to animals? What should I do with this gift?"

The fox's expression turned serious. "There is danger in the forest—a poacher who seeks to capture us for profit. We need someone to help us warn the others."

The weight of the fox's words settled heavily on Lila's shoulders. "I'll help!" she declared, determination surging within her.

Over the following days, Lila trained herself to harness her newfound ability. With the fox by her side, she learned to listen to the whispers of the woods. Birds guided her to hidden clearings where creatures gathered, and she began spreading the word about the poacher.

"Stay hidden, my friends," she urged them. "We must protect ourselves and warn others. I will find a way to stop this poacher!"

One evening, as the sun dipped below the horizon, Lila gathered a group of animals in the glade: deer, rabbits, birds, and even a wise old owl. They listened intently as she explained the poacher's threat.

"We need to be clever," Lila said. "If we work together, we can outsmart him."

The animals agreed, and they devised a plan. That night, they would create a diversion to draw the poacher's attention away from their homes. With Lila's guidance, the animals set to work. The rabbits dug trenches, the deer created false trails, and the birds would sing loud distractions.

As the moon rose high in the sky, the animals executed their plan. Lila watched from her hiding spot as the poacher, a burly man with a grizzled face, crept into the woods, his traps at the ready. Unbeknownst to him, Lila's furry and feathered friends were one step ahead.

The rabbits darted through the underbrush, creating a flurry of movement that caught the poacher's eye. He followed, grumbling in frustration as he stumbled over roots and branches. Meanwhile, the deer led him deeper into the forest, away from their true hiding spots.

But just as Lila thought their plan was working, she saw the poacher pull out a net, a wicked grin spreading across his face. "You can't escape me forever!" he shouted, lunging at the nearest rabbit.

"No!" Lila cried out, her heart racing. Without thinking, she dashed from her hiding place, calling upon her connection to the animals. "Stop him!" she shouted, her voice ringing with urgency.

In response, the fox sprang into action, leading the other animals in a coordinated effort. The birds swooped down, distracting the poacher, while the deer charged to block his path. Lila felt a surge of power as she realized that her voice was not just for talking; it was for commanding.

"Together!" Lila called, her heart pounding as she focused on the poacher. "You will not harm my friends!"

The animals moved in unison, creating a chaotic whirlwind around the poacher. Just as he was about to trap a rabbit, the fox lunged at his feet, causing him to stumble. With a cry of frustration, he turned to flee, abandoning his traps and nets.

As silence fell over the glade, the animals gathered around Lila, their eyes shining with gratitude. "You did it!" the fox exclaimed, panting slightly. "You saved us!"

Lila felt a wave of relief wash over her. "We did it together. I couldn't have done it without all of you."

But as she looked around at the grateful faces of her friends, a new realization struck her. "This gift... it's not just about communication. It's about understanding and working together."

The fox nodded, his expression serious. "Yes. The bond between us is what truly matters. When we listen to each other, we can overcome any challenge."

As dawn broke over the forest, Lila returned to the village, her heart full of hope and purpose. She would continue to protect the woods and its creatures, becoming a bridge between the worlds of humans and animals. And as she walked through the village, she shared her adventures, urging others to respect and protect the wilderness.

From that day forward, Lila became known as the Whisperer of the Wild, a guardian of harmony between nature and humanity. The lesson she had learned—of connection, understanding, and the strength of unity—remained etched in her heart. She knew that as long as they listened to one another, both the creatures of the forest and the people of Elderswood would thrive together.

The Bookshop of Wonders

In the heart of the bustling city of Eldridge, tucked between an old apothecary and a bakery that filled the streets with the scent of fresh bread, stood a quaint little bookshop known as "The Book Nook." It was a place where time seemed to slow down, where the air was heavy with the scent of aged paper and leather bindings. The shop was owned by an eccentric old woman named Agatha, who had a penchant for the whimsical and the arcane.

Agatha was rumored to have a magical touch; her books not only told stories but, in a way that few could comprehend, brought them to life. Locals often spoke of curious occurrences within the shop—books that whispered their tales, characters that danced across the pages, and stories that seemed to change with the reader's mood. But for many, it remained just a charming rumor.

One rainy afternoon, a weary traveler named Ethan stumbled into The Book Nook, seeking refuge from the downpour. Shaking off his coat, he took a moment to catch his breath as he admired the endless rows of books that lined the shelves. Each spine was adorned with intricate designs, inviting him to explore their depths.

"Welcome!" Agatha's voice rang out, bright and welcoming. She emerged from behind a towering stack of books, her silver hair a wild halo around her head. "What brings you to my humble shop?"

"I'm just trying to escape the rain," Ethan replied, his eyes scanning the titles. "But I've heard whispers that your books are... different."

"Oh, they are indeed," Agatha said, a knowing smile on her lips. "Each book contains a world waiting to be discovered. If you have an open mind, you might just find something extraordinary."

Intrigued, Ethan wandered through the aisles, his fingers grazing the spines as he searched for a story that called to him. His gaze landed on a dusty old tome, bound in deep blue leather with gilded lettering that read, "The Chronicles of Aetheria." Something about the book felt alive, tingling under his fingertips.

He pulled it from the shelf, and as he opened it, a warm light spilled out, enveloping him in its glow. Suddenly, the world around him blurred, and he felt himself being pulled into the pages.

When the light faded, Ethan found himself standing in a lush, vibrant forest. Sunlight filtered through the trees, casting playful shadows on the ground. Bewildered, he looked down to find he was no longer wearing his traveler's attire but a tunic made of soft fabric that smelled of the earth.

"Welcome to Aetheria, brave adventurer!" a melodious voice chimed.

Ethan turned to see a figure approaching—a graceful elf with long, flowing hair and eyes that sparkled like the stars. "I am Elyndra, keeper of the forest. You've arrived just in time; we need your help!"

"Help?" Ethan stammered, still trying to grasp the reality of his situation. "How can I help?"

"A darkness is spreading through our lands, corrupting the magic that sustains us," Elyndra explained. "Only a true-hearted adventurer can gather the three shards of light needed to restore balance. Will you aid us?"

Without fully understanding how he got there, Ethan nodded, a sense of purpose igniting within him. "I'll help!"

Elyndra led him deeper into the forest, where they encountered a fierce troll guarding the first shard. With quick thinking and the skills he had honed from countless stories, Ethan devised a clever ruse, distracting the troll with an illusion of treasure while Elyndra snatched the shard from its grasp.

As they continued their quest, Ethan and Elyndra faced challenges that tested their courage, wit, and teamwork. They traversed treacherous mountains, navigated enchanted rivers, and befriended mystical creatures who guided them on their path. Each trial brought them closer, forging a bond built on trust and camaraderie.

Finally, they reached the lair of a fearsome dragon, the guardian of the final shard. It loomed above them, scales glimmering like polished emeralds. "To claim the shard, you must prove your worth," the dragon rumbled, its voice echoing like thunder.

Ethan's heart raced. He had faced many trials, but this was different. He stepped forward, his voice steady. "What do you seek?"

"The truth of your heart," the dragon replied, narrowing its eyes. "Show me your courage."

With a deep breath, Ethan revealed his fears—his doubts about himself, his feelings of inadequacy, and the desire to belong. The dragon listened intently, and with each word, the air shimmered with energy.

"You possess true courage," the dragon said, its voice softening. "You have faced your inner demons. You may claim the shard."

As Ethan grasped the final shard, a brilliant light enveloped him and Elyndra. They returned to the heart of the forest, where the shards merged into a radiant orb, dispelling the darkness and restoring balance to Aetheria.

With their quest complete, Ethan felt a pull again, the familiar warmth surrounding him. As the light faded, he found himself back in The Book Nook, the old tome still open in his hands.

Agatha stood nearby, a knowing smile on her face. "You found the courage within you, didn't you?"

Ethan looked up, astonished. "It felt so real. I didn't just read a story; I lived it."

"That is the magic of this place," Agatha explained. "Stories are not just tales; they are mirrors reflecting our truths. When we embrace them, we discover who we truly are."

Ethan closed the book, a smile spreading across his face. "Thank you for showing me that. I've learned that the greatest adventures are those that help us grow."

As he left the shop, the rain had cleared, and the sun shone brightly. The lesson he had learned resonated within him—a reminder that every story, whether real or imagined, has the power to reveal our deepest truths and help us navigate the complexities of our own lives. And sometimes, the greatest treasure lies not in the adventures we seek but in the understanding we gain along the way.

The Blade of Destiny

In the rugged hills of the Kingdom of Eldarwyn, where the mountains scraped the sky and rivers flowed like silver ribbons, there was a blacksmith named Kaelan. Renowned for his craftsmanship, he forged tools and weapons that were said to be blessed by the very spirits of the forge. Yet, despite his skills, Kaelan felt unfulfilled, haunted by dreams of a blade that could alter fate itself.

For years, whispers of a legendary sword known as "Fate's Edge" echoed through taverns and marketplaces. Crafted from a rare metal found only in the depths of the Cursed Caverns, the sword was said to possess the power to change destiny with a single swing. Many had attempted to create such a weapon, but none had succeeded. The elusive metal was both precious and dangerous, guarded by the very essence of fate.

One stormy evening, a cloaked figure entered Kaelan's forge, water dripping from the hem of their cloak. "I seek your skill, blacksmith," the stranger said, their voice low and commanding. "I need you to forge a weapon that can reshape destiny."

Kaelan raised an eyebrow, intrigued yet cautious. "I've heard tales of such a sword, but it is a perilous endeavor. The metal required comes from the Cursed Caverns, and many who venture there never return."

The stranger stepped closer, revealing sharp features and eyes that glimmered with determination. "I have the means to acquire the metal. In return for your skill, I seek to change the course of my life."

Intrigued, Kaelan agreed. Together, they journeyed to the Cursed Caverns, their path illuminated only by the flickering light of torches. Inside the dark and twisting passages, they faced chilling winds and strange echoes, as if the very walls held secrets of the past.

After what felt like an eternity, they stumbled upon a chamber filled with glimmering ore, pulsating with a soft blue light. "This is it," the stranger said, excitement lacing their voice. "Collect as much as you can."

Kaelan gathered the ore, feeling its power radiate through his fingers. As they turned to leave, however, a low growl reverberated through the cavern. A colossal guardian, a creature made of shadows and ancient magic, emerged from the darkness. "Who dares disturb my slumber?" it roared, its eyes glowing with an otherworldly light.

Panic surged through Kaelan, but the stranger stepped forward, their presence unwavering. "We mean no harm. We seek only the metal to forge a weapon of destiny."

The guardian's gaze narrowed. "To forge such a weapon, you must prove your worth. Answer my riddle, or face the consequences."

Kaelan nodded, steeling himself. "What is the riddle?"

"Only those who embrace their past can shape their future. What is the one thing that binds them together?" the guardian asked.

The question struck deep within Kaelan's heart. He thought of his own life—the regrets, the choices, the paths he had taken. "Memories," he finally answered, his voice steady. "Memories bind our past to our future."

The guardian paused, considering his answer. "You speak truth. You may take the metal, but remember: the blade you forge will hold the weight of your memories. Use it wisely."

With the ore secured, Kaelan and the stranger returned to the forge. For days and nights, he worked tirelessly, hammering and shaping the metal, pouring his heart into the creation of the sword. As he worked, he felt an unusual connection to the blade, as if it was awakening to the essence of destiny itself.

Finally, the sword was complete. It gleamed with a fierce, ethereal light, the hilt adorned with intricate engravings that seemed to shimmer and dance. Kaelan stepped back, breathless at the beauty of his creation.

"Fate's Edge," the stranger murmured, awe in their voice. "With this, I can reshape my destiny."

But Kaelan hesitated. "What are your intentions? Changing fate can have unforeseen consequences."

The stranger smiled, revealing a glint of ambition in their eyes. "I will no longer be bound by the chains of my past. I will take control of my life!"

As they raised the sword, Kaelan felt a sudden chill wash over him. "Wait! You must remember—this blade does not merely alter fate; it reflects the wielder's true desires. If your heart is consumed by ambition, it could bring ruin."

The stranger scoffed, their confidence unwavering. "I know what I want. I'm ready."

But as the blade ignited with power, a dark shadow enveloped the chamber. The walls trembled, and the air crackled with magic. Suddenly, the sword began to pulse, drawing energy from the stranger. "No!" Kaelan shouted, reaching for them. "You must let go!"

The sword surged, and the stranger's face twisted in agony. "I... can't!"

In a blinding flash of light, the blade shattered, sending shards flying across the room. The stranger collapsed, gasping for breath as the darkness receded. Kaelan rushed to their side, fear clawing at his heart.

"What happened?" the stranger murmured, their voice weak.

"The sword reflected your desires, and your ambition nearly consumed you," Kaelan said, his voice steady but filled with concern. "You sought power without considering the consequences."

As the dust settled, the remnants of the sword shimmered softly on the ground. The guardian's voice echoed in Kaelan's mind: "The blade holds the weight of memories."

Realization struck him like lightning. "You must embrace your past, not seek to escape it. The true strength lies in acceptance, not ambition."

With newfound clarity, the stranger nodded, their expression softening. "I understand now. I was blinded by my desire for control."

As dawn broke outside the forge, Kaelan and the stranger emerged, forever changed. They had faced the darkness together and learned that altering fate required more than just power—it required wisdom, acceptance, and the courage to confront one's own truth.

The lesson lingered in the air, a reminder that while we all wish to shape our destinies, it is often our memories and choices that guide us toward the future we seek. And in that understanding, both Kaelan and the stranger found a path not just to survive but to thrive, united by the bond of their shared journey.

The Sorcerers of Seasons

In the enchanting Kingdom of Verenthia, the four seasons were not merely a passage of time but the delicate balance of nature, carefully maintained by four powerful sorcerers. Each sorcerer wielded dominion over their respective season, crafting the beauty of the land through their magic. There was Aurelius, the Sorcerer of Spring, whose gentle touch coaxed flowers from the earth; Seraphina, the Sorceress of Summer, who basked the land in warmth and light; Thorne, the Sorcerer of Autumn, whose hands painted the leaves in hues of gold and crimson; and Winter's guardian, Eira, who enveloped the kingdom in a serene blanket of snow.

For generations, the sorcerers worked in harmony, their powers intertwined, ensuring that the seasons flowed seamlessly from one to another. Yet, beneath the surface of this idyllic kingdom, tensions simmered. Eira, weary of being seen as the cold, distant sorceress, began to resent the warmer seasons and their ability to bring joy and life to the land.

One fateful day, the balance shattered. Eira, driven by her desire to be recognized, devised a plan. She would unleash an eternal winter upon Verenthia, forcing the other sorcerers to acknowledge her power. As the sun rose, the air grew frigid, and snow began to fall in thick, heavy flakes, blanketing the kingdom in icy silence.

The other sorcerers sensed the disturbance in the balance of nature. Aurelius gathered the spring flowers, calling them to bloom early to combat the chill. Seraphina summoned her warmth to thaw the ground, and Thorne tried to bring color back to the trees with a golden hue. But Eira's magic was too strong. The frost crept into their realms, suffocating their efforts.

"Eira, you must stop this!" Aurelius pleaded, his voice filled with concern. "You are disrupting the natural order!"

"Why should I listen to you?" Eira snapped, her icy gaze piercing. "You all take the glory while I am relegated to the shadows. I will show you the true power of winter!"

The three sorcerers rallied together, pooling their magic to counter Eira's. They formed a protective barrier, but the winter's grip tightened. Snowstorms raged, and life began to wither under the relentless cold.

In a desperate attempt to save Verenthia, Aurelius hatched a plan. "We must confront Eira together, not as rivals but as allies. We need to show her that the seasons rely on each other. Without spring, summer cannot thrive; without autumn, winter cannot be born anew."

Reluctantly, Seraphina and Thorne agreed. They journeyed to Eira's icy palace, a fortress of glistening ice and snow, standing defiantly against the swirling winds. As they entered, they found Eira seated on a throne of frost, surrounded by howling winds.

"Why have you come?" Eira's voice echoed, cold and harsh.

"We come to help you," Thorne said, stepping forward. "We understand your pain, but this isn't the way. We need balance."

"Balance?" Eira laughed bitterly. "You think I want to be balanced? I want to be respected!"

Seraphina, taking a deep breath, replied, "We respect you, Eira. We've always respected you. But winter is part of a cycle, not the whole. Let us show you how the seasons can coexist."

With a wave of her hand, Seraphina summoned warmth, creating a beautiful spring scene in the throne room. Flowers bloomed, and warmth radiated through the air. "Feel this joy, Eira. It doesn't take away from your beauty; it enhances it."

A flicker of doubt crossed Eira's icy facade. "But what if I'm left behind?"

"Winter is necessary for spring," Aurelius interjected. "Your season nurtures the earth, allowing life to rest and regenerate. Without you, there would be no balance."

Slowly, the frost surrounding Eira began to melt, revealing the vibrant colors that had been hidden beneath the ice. The warmth seeped into her heart, awakening memories of laughter and life.

"Do you not remember the beauty of the seasons working together?" Thorne asked gently. "You are part of a greater whole."

As the trio continued to share their warmth and memories, Eira felt her heart thawing. She had been so consumed by her desire for recognition that she had forgotten the joy of unity. Finally, tears welled in her eyes, and she whispered, "I just wanted to be seen."

Embracing her vulnerability, Eira stepped down from her throne. "I see now that my desire for power led me astray. I do not wish to be alone in my reign." With a wave of her hand, the raging storms subsided, and the ice around them melted, revealing a landscape rich with color and life.

With Eira's newfound understanding, the four sorcerers joined hands, pooling their magic together. They created a magnificent spectacle of the seasons, where spring blossomed into summer, yielding to autumn's gentle embrace before surrendering to winter's serene touch.

The kingdom of Verenthia thrived once more, a place where the seasons danced in harmony. Eira learned that her presence was not diminished by her friends; instead, it became a vital part of the cycle of life.

As the sun set over the kingdom, the sorcerers stood together, united by their differences and strengthened by their bonds. They had learned that true power lay not in the desire for recognition but in the willingness to embrace one another's strengths.

In the end, the lesson resonated throughout Eldarwyn: that unity in diversity creates a richness in life that surpasses the need for individual glory. Each season, like each individual, has its place and purpose, and together they weave the tapestry of existence.

The Heart's Divide

In the kingdom of Eldoria, where emerald valleys kissed the sky and silver rivers flowed like veins through the land, a formidable warrior named Kaelin served Queen Isolde. Clad in gleaming armor and known for her unmatched skill in battle, she was the queen's most trusted protector. But beneath her fierce exterior lay a heart torn between duty and desire.

Kaelin had sworn an oath of loyalty to Isolde, a queen who had brought peace and prosperity to the kingdom after years of war. Her strength and charisma inspired devotion in her subjects, and Kaelin was no exception. Yet, over time, she found herself captivated by someone outside the court—Elara, a talented healer with an ethereal beauty that seemed to reflect the very light of the stars.

The two had met during a battle where Elara tended to the wounded, her gentle touch healing even the gravest injuries. Their paths had crossed often since, and as Kaelin fought to protect the queen, her heart longed for the healer who brought comfort and hope to those in pain.

As tensions rose in the kingdom, a dark threat loomed on the horizon. Rumors of an invasion by the neighboring realm of Thalor reached the palace, and the queen prepared for war. "We must be ready to defend our land," Isolde declared in a council meeting, her eyes fierce and determined. "I will not let our people suffer again."

Kaelin's loyalty to Isolde burned bright, yet her heart ached for Elara, who had been trying to rally support for the refugees who would be caught in the crossfire of war. "My queen," Kaelin said, her voice steady but laced with emotion, "we cannot ignore the suffering of innocents. If we go to war, many will perish."

Isolde's gaze turned cold, a flicker of frustration crossing her face. "Do you question my judgment, Kaelin? The safety of our kingdom comes first."

In that moment, Kaelin felt the weight of her loyalties pressing down upon her. "I do not question your judgment, but I must also consider my heart. There is a way to protect our people without resorting to violence."

As the days passed, Kaelin wrestled with her emotions. She sought solace in the company of Elara, sharing her fears about the impending war and the queen's unwavering resolve. "I cannot abandon my duty," Kaelin confessed, her voice breaking. "But my heart longs to stand beside you, to fight for those who cannot fight for themselves."

Elara took her hands, warmth radiating between them. "You must follow your heart, Kaelin. True loyalty is not only to the crown but also to your beliefs and the love you carry within you. You can be a warrior and still protect those you care for."

The night before the queen's army was to march, Kaelin faced her dilemma. She could lead her fellow warriors into battle, or she could heed Elara's words and seek a path of peace. Torn between the two, she resolved to speak with Isolde one last time.

In the dim light of the queen's chambers, Kaelin stood before Isolde, her heart racing. "My queen, I urge you to reconsider your approach. We can negotiate with Thalor. We do not have to engage in bloodshed."

Isolde's expression hardened, her regal demeanor unwavering. "You wish to negotiate with those who would invade us? They do not seek peace; they seek power. You are a warrior, Kaelin! Stand with me."

"Yet I also carry the burden of my heart," Kaelin replied, desperation tinging her voice. "I cannot follow you into battle if it means sacrificing innocent lives."

Isolde's gaze softened, but her resolve remained firm. "I cannot accept this weakness. If you abandon your duty, you abandon me."

In that moment, Kaelin knew she had to choose. "I cannot forsake who I am for fear of your judgment. I must follow my heart, even if it leads me away from you."

With a heavy heart, Kaelin left the queen's chambers, tears brimming in her eyes. She hurried to Elara's sanctuary in the woods, where the healer awaited her. "I cannot go to war, Elara. I must stand for peace, even if it means losing everything."

Elara's face illuminated with understanding. "Then let us find a way together. We can gather support from the villages, unite the people against the bloodshed."

As dawn broke, Kaelin and Elara set out to rally the villagers, sharing their vision of peace. They traveled from hamlet to hamlet, their words igniting a spark of hope in the hearts of those who had lost faith in a better future. The people rallied, and soon, a movement for peace grew stronger than any sword could wield.

But as they returned to the capital, a messenger approached, breathless with urgency. "The queen's forces are on the move! They march to meet Thalor's army!"

Kaelin's heart sank, realizing the impending conflict. "We must reach Isolde before it's too late!"

The two women raced to the castle, but when they arrived, the air crackled with tension. Soldiers stood ready, weapons drawn, and the atmosphere was heavy with anticipation. Kaelin pushed through the crowd, her voice rising above the noise. "Isolde! Stop! You cannot fight!"

The queen turned, her eyes fierce. "Stand down, Kaelin. This is my decision."

"No!" Kaelin pleaded, desperation coloring her words. "We can negotiate! We have the support of the people! We can end this without bloodshed!"

The soldiers hesitated, glancing between their queen and the warrior who had always stood by her side. Kaelin's heart raced as she felt the weight of her choices. She took a deep breath, summoning all the courage she had. "Isolde, I know you are strong and capable, but true strength lies not in fighting but in unity and compassion."

Silence enveloped the crowd as the queen's fierce expression faltered, her gaze shifting from anger to contemplation. "You would turn your back on me?" she whispered, hurt evident in her voice.

"No," Kaelin replied softly. "I choose to stand for love and peace, not just for myself but for everyone, including you."

After a long pause, Isolde stepped forward, her resolve crumbling. "What have I become? If I cannot listen to the hearts of my people, am I worthy to lead?"

The tension broke as the queen's voice softened, a reluctant acceptance dawning on her. "I will hear you, Kaelin. We will seek peace, but it must come from a place of strength."

As the sun rose higher in the sky, the warriors put down their weapons, and a new dialogue began between the two kingdoms. Kaelin stood beside Isolde and Elara, united by their vision of a brighter future. In that moment, she realized that true loyalty lay not in blind obedience but in the courage to speak one's truth.

From that day forward, the kingdom thrived, bound not just by the loyalty of its warriors but by the strength of its heart. And as Kaelin embraced her role as a peacekeeper, she understood that love and courage could forge a path to a future worth fighting for—a lesson that would echo through the ages, reminding all that the heart's voice is often the strongest weapon of all.

The Whispering Oak

In the heart of Eldergrove, a mystical forest brimming with vibrant life and ancient magic, stood a colossal oak tree known as Elysia. Towering above the other trees, its gnarled branches spread wide, and its leaves shimmered with a luminescent green hue. Elysia was no ordinary tree; it was sentient, a guardian of ancient secrets and the wisdom of the ages. The villagers of Eldergrove revered Elysia, visiting often to seek counsel or simply to sit beneath its protective canopy, feeling the comfort of its presence.

One such villager was Elara, a curious young woman with a thirst for knowledge and adventure. She often spent hours near Elysia, entranced by the stories the tree seemed to whisper through the rustling of its leaves. She had heard tales of the secrets the tree guarded—knowledge of lost civilizations, the art of healing, and the balance of nature. But what intrigued her most was the legend of the Tree's Heart, a magical gem hidden deep within the tree that granted the power to unveil the truth behind any mystery.

One fateful evening, as the sun dipped below the horizon and painted the sky in hues of orange and purple, Elara approached Elysia with a heavy heart. "I seek your wisdom, dear Elysia," she began, her voice barely above a whisper. "I want to know the truth about my mother. She left when I was young, and I wish to understand why."

Elysia's leaves rustled softly, as if pondering her request. "The truth you seek is not simple, Elara. Are you prepared for what you might find?"

Elara took a deep breath, steeling herself. "I am. I need to know."

With a gentle tremor, Elysia's trunk shifted, revealing a hidden hollow. Inside, glimmering in the twilight, lay the Tree's Heart—a radiant gem pulsating with light. "To know the truth, you must first embrace the heart of the forest," Elysia intoned, "but be warned: knowledge can be both a blessing and a burden."

Reaching into the hollow, Elara grasped the gem, feeling a surge of energy coursing through her. As she held it, visions flooded her mind—images of her mother laughing, dancing in the rain, and then, suddenly, a shadow creeping into their lives. She saw glimpses of fear, anger, and the moment her mother chose to leave. The memories were raw and vivid, leaving Elara breathless.

"Why did she leave?" Elara cried out, the pain of those memories crashing over her like a wave.

The Tree's Heart pulsed in her hand, and the visions changed. She saw her mother standing before a dark figure, a sorcerer whose eyes glowed with malice. "To protect you, I must go," her mother's voice echoed. "He seeks the power of the Tree's Heart for himself."

Elara's heart raced as the realization struck her. "She left to keep me safe... but from what?"

With a heavy sigh, Elysia replied, "Your mother sacrificed her happiness to shield you from a darkness that would have consumed you both. She believed that if she severed the bond, the sorcerer would be unable to find you."

As the visions faded, Elara felt a mix of gratitude and sorrow. "But she could have stayed! We could have faced it together!"

"Sometimes, love means making the hardest choices," Elysia explained gently. "Your mother's strength lay in her sacrifice. To protect you, she believed this was her only option."

Elara's mind swirled with emotions—anger at her mother for leaving, sorrow for the life they could have shared, and an overwhelming sense of loss. Yet beneath it all, a spark of understanding began to take root. "I see now," she murmured, her voice steadying. "She loved me enough to let me go."

Elysia's branches swayed, as if nodding in agreement. "Understanding is the first step toward healing, Elara. It is a powerful gift."

But Elara wasn't finished. "But I want to stop the sorcerer! I want to protect others like her!"

With renewed determination, she looked back at the gem. "How can I use the Tree's Heart to confront this darkness?"

Elysia's voice resonated through the clearing. "The Heart holds the knowledge of the past, but it is your courage and love that will guide you. To confront the sorcerer, you must gather allies and forge connections with those who share your vision."

With Elysia's wisdom as her guide, Elara made a plan. She would return to the village and rally those who had suffered under the sorcerer's reign, uniting their strengths to confront the darkness. Inspired by her mother's love and sacrifice, she felt empowered to protect her home.

In the days that followed, Elara shared her revelations with the villagers, recounting her mother's bravery and the threat that still loomed over them. With their hearts ignited by her words, a group of warriors, healers, and mages gathered, ready to stand against the sorcerer.

The final confrontation took place in the shadowy depths of the forest, where the sorcerer had taken refuge. With the Tree's Heart glowing at her side, Elara led her allies into battle. Together, they faced the sorcerer, who underestimated the power of their unity.

As the clash of magic and steel filled the air, Elara's heart surged with determination. She drew on the strength of her mother's sacrifice and the love that had united them all. In a moment of clarity, she used the Tree's Heart to channel the memories of those who had suffered and to amplify their collective power.

With a blinding flash, the sorcerer was overwhelmed by the force of their unity, banished from the realm, and with him, the shadow that had plagued them.

As the dust settled, Elara stood among her friends, her heart swelling with pride and relief. "We did it," she whispered, tears of joy streaming down her face.

In the aftermath, she returned to Elysia, the Tree's Heart still pulsing softly in her hands. "Thank you for your guidance," she said, her voice filled with gratitude.

Elysia's leaves rustled gently, and a warm breeze enveloped Elara. "You have learned that love transcends even the greatest sacrifices. Your mother's legacy lives on in you, and you have the power to shape a brighter future."

With newfound clarity, Elara understood that she would carry her mother's spirit with her, honoring her sacrifice by fighting for the love and unity she believed in.

And so, the Kingdom of Eldoria thrived, protected not just by the strength of its warriors, but by the bonds of love that had been forged through understanding and shared purpose. In the heart of the forest, Elysia stood tall, a reminder of the secrets of the past and the power of the human heart.

The Petals of Elyndra

In a secluded glade, far beyond the bustling villages and sprawling towns of the human realm, lay a mystical flower known as the Elyndra Bloom. This rare flower was said to bloom only once every hundred years, and when it did, it unveiled the entrance to a hidden fairy kingdom nestled within its luminous petals. The stories of the Elyndra Bloom echoed through the ages, tales of magic, enchantment, and the elusive fairies that guarded ancient secrets.

One fateful day, a curious herbalist named Mira stumbled upon the glade while foraging for rare herbs. With chestnut hair and a heart full of wonder, she had spent years studying the flora of the realm, always seeking the extraordinary. As she entered the glade, her breath caught in her throat at the sight before her: the Elyndra Bloom stood proudly, its petals shimmering with iridescent colors, beckoning her closer.

Mira approached cautiously, feeling an inexplicable pull toward the flower. As she reached out to touch its soft petals, the ground trembled beneath her feet. The Elyndra Bloom began to unfurl, revealing a swirling portal within its core. With a mixture of trepidation and excitement, Mira stepped forward, curiosity overriding her caution.

As she passed through the portal, she was enveloped in a kaleidoscope of colors and light. When the brilliance faded, she found herself in a breathtaking realm—a fairy kingdom alive with vibrant flowers, luminescent streams, and fluttering creatures that danced in the air. The scent of sweet nectar filled her lungs, and the sound of laughter echoed through the vibrant landscape.

"Mira!" a voice chimed, drawing her attention. A small fairy with delicate wings and sparkling eyes approached her, a smile illuminating her face. "Welcome to Elyndra! We've been waiting for someone like you."

"Who are you?" Mira asked, still in awe of the beauty around her.

"I am Faye, a guardian of the Elyndra Bloom," the fairy explained. "You possess a rare spirit, one that connects deeply with nature. That's why you found us."

As Faye led Mira through the kingdom, she learned of the fairies' delicate balance with nature. They tended to the flowers, guided the seasons, and safeguarded the magic of the realm. Mira felt a deep sense of belonging among them, a connection she had never experienced in her solitary life as an herbalist.

Days turned into weeks as Mira immersed herself in the fairy kingdom, learning their ways and sharing her knowledge of herbs and healing. The fairies adored her, and Mira found joy in their laughter and camaraderie. Yet, as the time of the Elyndra Bloom's closing approached, a sense of dread crept into her heart. She knew she would have to choose: stay in this enchanting world or return to her own, where the mundane awaited her.

One evening, as the sun dipped below the horizon, casting a golden glow over the kingdom, Faye approached Mira with a worried expression. "Mira, I must speak with you. There's a darkness threatening our realm. The magic of the Elyndra Bloom is waning, and without its protection, our kingdom will be lost."

"What can we do?" Mira asked, her heart pounding with concern.

"There's an ancient spell that can strengthen the Bloom's magic," Faye explained, her voice steady. "But it requires a rare ingredient—the Heart of the Earth, a gem hidden deep within the Enchanted Cavern. Only someone with a pure heart can retrieve it."

Mira felt a surge of determination. "I will find it. I can't let this kingdom fall."

Faye's eyes sparkled with gratitude. "Thank you, Mira. But the cavern is treacherous. You must be careful."

The next morning, Mira set off toward the Enchanted Cavern, her heart filled with purpose. The journey was perilous, filled with twisting paths and ominous shadows. As she delved deeper into the cavern, she faced obstacles that tested her resolve—illusions that played on her fears and creatures that sought to deter her.

But with each challenge, Mira remembered the joy of the fairy kingdom and the bond she had forged with its inhabitants. Summoning her courage, she pushed through the darkness, until she finally reached a shimmering chamber. In the center of the room lay the Heart of the Earth, a radiant gem pulsating with energy.

As she approached the gem, a voice echoed through the cavern. "Who dares claim the Heart?"

Mira steeled herself, knowing she had to face this final challenge. "I seek to protect the Elyndra Bloom and its magic. I wish to save the fairy kingdom!"

The guardian of the gem emerged—a massive earth spirit, its form shifting like stone and soil. "To claim the Heart, you must prove your intentions are true. Speak your heart's desire."

Mira took a deep breath. "I desire to protect the magic of the fairies, to ensure their world thrives. I have found a home among them, and I cannot bear the thought of their suffering."

The earth spirit studied her, its eyes piercing through her soul. "Your intentions are pure. You may take the Heart."

With the gem in hand, Mira felt a surge of warmth and power course through her. She raced back to the fairy kingdom, the gem glowing brightly. As she entered the realm, the fairies gathered around her, hope shining in their eyes.

Mira placed the Heart of the Earth at the base of the Elyndra Bloom. Instantly, a wave of energy rippled through the flower, its petals opening wide and glowing with renewed strength. The magic pulsed and spread, weaving through the kingdom, pushing back the darkness.

As the celebration erupted around her, Mira felt a pang of longing. She had forged bonds of love and friendship here, but she also had a life waiting for her back in the human realm. Faye noticed her contemplative expression and approached, concern etched on her face.

"Mira, what troubles you?"

"I've found my place among you, but I know I must return to my world," Mira confessed, her voice thick with emotion. "I can't stay."

Faye smiled, understanding flooding her features. "Your heart belongs to both worlds. You can carry the magic of Elyndra with you. Remember, the love you've cultivated here will always be part of you."

As the sun set over the kingdom, Mira felt the warmth of the fairies' love surrounding her. With the magic of the Elyndra Bloom still flowing through her, she stepped back through the portal, carrying with her the strength of the heart she had nurtured in both realms.

In the years that followed, Mira became a protector of nature in her own world, healing the land and fostering growth wherever she went. The lessons of love, courage, and the intertwining of worlds shaped her life, a testament to the bond she had formed with the fairies.

And every now and then, when the moon was full and the air was still, she could hear the whispers of the Elyndra Bloom calling her home, a reminder that magic exists wherever love is nurtured.

Beneath the Shadows

In the sprawling city of Thaloria, where stone towers pierced the sky and cobblestone streets thrummed with life, few knew of the ancient secrets hidden beneath their feet. Below the bustling surface lay an intricate network of tunnels and chambers, home to a mystical race known as the Glynari—creatures of light and shadow, bound to the earth but forever longing for the sun.

The Glynari were ethereal beings, their forms shifting like smoke and light, with skin that glimmered in hues of silver and blue. They were the guardians of the city's life force, drawing energy from the roots of the ancient trees that thrived in the depths of the earth. Their magic was intertwined with the very essence of Thaloria, but over the years, the connection had grown weak as the city above expanded, consuming more and more of the natural world.

Elowen, a young Glynari, felt the change acutely. Her connection to the roots and the light that flowed from them was fading, and with it, the vitality of her people. "We must do something," she urged her fellow Glynari during a gathering in the underground chamber, where glowing crystals lit the room with a soft luminescence.

"The city above is a lost cause," grumbled Corwin, a skeptical elder. "They have forgotten us and the magic that sustains them. What can we do?"

"Perhaps we can remind them," Elowen suggested, her voice steady with determination. "If we can restore our bond with the city, we can reignite the magic. I know a way to reach the surface."

Intrigued but cautious, the Glynari listened as Elowen explained her plan. She would use the last vestiges of their magic to manifest a shimmering gateway—a portal that would allow her to walk among the people of Thaloria. "If I can show them the beauty of our world, they may understand how to help us."

Despite their doubts, the Glynari agreed, and together they channeled their energy into the portal. With a flash of light, Elowen stepped through, her heart racing with excitement and fear.

The bustling streets of Thaloria were a cacophony of sounds and scents, a vibrant tapestry of life that overwhelmed her senses. Elowen marveled at the colorful stalls and the laughter of children playing. Yet, as she observed the people, she noticed their hurried pace, their faces etched with worry. They seemed unaware of the magic that thrummed beneath the city, a magic that connected them all.

Determined to make her presence known, Elowen wandered into a marketplace. She found a small gathering of artists and musicians, their talents capturing the attention of passersby. With a wave of her hand, she conjured a gentle breeze, and vibrant flowers began to bloom from the cobblestones, swirling around the performers.

Gasps of astonishment filled the air as people paused to witness the enchanting display. "What is this magic?" a street artist exclaimed, his eyes wide. "Where did it come from?"

"I am Elowen, a guardian of the Glynari," she announced, her voice carrying over the crowd. "I come to remind you of the magic that lies beneath your feet, the bond we share with the earth."

As she spoke, Elowen shared stories of her people and the ancient trees that sustained them. She painted a picture of the vibrant world below, where life flourished in harmony. Her words resonated, and the crowd began to listen, captivated by the vision she conjured.

But not everyone was enchanted. A figure emerged from the crowd, a merchant with a hard expression. "Why should we care about the underground? We have our own lives to worry about. You're nothing but a trickster!" He scoffed, turning his back.

Elowen felt a wave of disappointment wash over her. "You don't see the connection, do you? Our worlds are intertwined. If you neglect the roots, the tree will wither."

With that, a surge of energy rushed through her, and she manifested a vision of the Glynari kingdom—its beauty, its magic, and its plight. The crowd gasped as they witnessed the vibrant colors and the lush landscapes beneath the city, but the vision soon darkened, showing the roots shriveling and the light fading.

The merchant's demeanor shifted, and his eyes widened in realization. "What have we done?"

Just then, the ground trembled, and a rift opened in the cobblestones. A surge of energy erupted, sending waves of warmth and light through the air. The Glynari appeared, their forms shimmering and dancing among the startled townsfolk.

"Together, we can heal this," Elowen said, her heart racing with hope. "But it must begin with understanding and respect for the earth."

The townsfolk, once skeptical, now stood in awe. They could feel the magic pulsing around them, the bond between their world and the Glynari becoming palpable. Slowly, they began to talk to one another, discussing ways to integrate their lives with the magical world beneath their feet.

As the sun dipped below the horizon, painting the sky with hues of orange and purple, Elowen felt a sense of fulfillment. She had sparked a conversation, igniting a flicker of hope.

But as the night deepened, the merchant stepped forward once more. "I may have been blind before, but I see now. Let us build a bridge—a literal and metaphorical one between our worlds."

And so, the people of Thaloria and the Glynari began to work together, planting trees that connected the underground kingdom to the surface, creating parks and gardens that celebrated their shared existence. The bond between the two worlds flourished, reviving the roots of magic that had been neglected for too long.

As Elowen returned to the Glynari, she realized that the lesson she had learned transcended the boundaries of her journey. It was not just about the magic that flowed through the land, but the understanding that true strength lies in connection—between people, between worlds, and between the past and the future.

And from that day on, both the city and the kingdom below thrived, bound by the magic of their shared existence, a testament to the power of understanding and unity in a world where every heartbeat mattered.

The Orphan's Crown

In the bustling town of Rivermoor, nestled between verdant hills and winding rivers, lived an orphan named Finn. With tousled hair and an ever-present spark of curiosity in his eyes, Finn spent his days scavenging for scraps and exploring the cobblestone streets. He had learned to survive on his own, but deep down, he longed for a sense of belonging and purpose that always seemed just out of reach.

As the townsfolk went about their lives, they often spoke of a long-lost royal family, vanished under mysterious circumstances. Legends circulated about a magical throne hidden in the ancient ruins of Eldoria, said to hold the power to restore balance to the kingdom. Yet for Finn, those tales were nothing more than fanciful stories meant to entertain children and distract them from their harsh realities.

One fateful evening, while rummaging through a forgotten alley, Finn stumbled upon an ornate box half-buried in the dirt. Intrigued, he pried it open, revealing an intricately carved amulet that pulsed with a soft, golden light. The moment he touched it, a surge of warmth coursed through him, and strange symbols began to glow on the surface of the amulet. A voice echoed in his mind, urging him to follow the path of destiny.

Finn's heart raced as he clutched the amulet, feeling an inexplicable connection to it. He was drawn to the nearby woods, where ancient trees whispered secrets and shadows danced in the twilight. The deeper he ventured, the more he sensed that the forest held answers to questions he hadn't even thought to ask.

After what felt like hours of wandering, Finn reached the ruins of Eldoria, their majestic stonework half-hidden by vines and moss. In the center of the crumbling courtyard stood a magnificent throne, overgrown with wildflowers and shimmering in the fading light. The amulet around his neck began to pulse in response to the throne, and Finn felt an overwhelming urge to approach.

As he neared the throne, the symbols on the amulet flared brightly, illuminating the ruins. Finn hesitated, doubts swirling in his mind. "What if this is just a trick?" he whispered to himself. But as he stood before the throne, he felt a sense of belonging he had never known.

With a deep breath, Finn took his place on the throne. As he settled into the seat, the ground trembled, and a whirlwind of energy enveloped him. Visions flooded his mind—images of a royal family, a kingdom in turmoil, and a young boy resembling him, holding the same amulet. The truth washed over him like a tidal wave: he was the last heir to the throne of Eldoria.

"You have returned, heir of Eldoria," a voice boomed, resonating through the ruins. Finn looked around, startled, as a shimmering figure appeared before him—a majestic spirit, clad in robes that flowed like water. "I am Aeloria, the guardian of this realm. Your family once ruled with wisdom and compassion, but darkness has encroached upon our land since their disappearance."

"What darkness?" Finn asked, his heart racing. "And what do you want from me?"

"The throne is not merely a seat of power; it is a symbol of hope and unity. You possess the potential to restore balance to our kingdom," Aeloria explained. "But to do so, you must first confront the shadows that threaten our world."

Finn's mind raced. He had spent his life surviving on the fringes of society, unprepared for the weight of a kingdom on his shoulders. "I'm just an orphan! I don't know how to be a king."

"True strength lies not in experience but in the courage to embrace your destiny," Aeloria said gently. "You must gather allies, seek the knowledge of your ancestors, and learn the magic that flows through this land."

With a newfound sense of purpose, Finn rose from the throne, determination coursing through his veins. "I will do it. I will reclaim my rightful place and protect this kingdom."

As he stepped away from the throne, the amulet glowed brightly, illuminating the path before him. Finn felt a connection to the land, as if the very earth beneath him was urging him forward. He began his journey, rallying villagers who had once looked down on him and gaining their trust by showing kindness and bravery.

With each ally he gathered, Finn learned more about the magic of Eldoria. He discovered forgotten spells and ancient wisdom, slowly transforming from an orphan into a leader. But as his power grew, so did the shadows that sought to extinguish the light he was bringing.

One fateful night, as Finn and his allies prepared to confront the dark force threatening Eldoria, a betrayal struck. A trusted friend, jealous of Finn's rapid rise, revealed their plan to the enemy. The forces of darkness descended upon them, intent on claiming the throne for themselves.

In the midst of chaos, Finn realized that all his strength meant nothing without trust and unity. With the amulet glowing fiercely, he called upon his allies to stand together. "We may not have the strength of an army, but we have each other! We fight for the light, for our home, and for each other!"

As they fought back against the darkness, Finn felt the true power of the throne awaken within him. The amulet pulsed with energy, and together with his allies, they pushed back against the shadows, reclaiming their home.

In the aftermath of the battle, as dawn broke over the horizon, Finn stood among his friends, breathing in the fresh air. "We did it!" he exclaimed, tears of joy in his eyes.

"You did it, Finn," Aeloria's spirit appeared once more, her voice soft yet powerful. "You embraced your destiny, and in doing so, you have become the true king of Eldoria."

Finn smiled, but he understood the lesson he had learned. It was not the title of king that mattered, but the bonds forged in unity and trust. He had transformed from an orphan into a leader not through blood but through love and connection.

As the kingdom thrived once more, Finn vowed to rule with compassion and humility, honoring the legacy of those who had come before him. The whispers of the wind carried the tale of the orphan who became a king, a reminder that true power lies not in status but in the strength of the heart.

The Doorway in the Meadow

In the quaint village of Eldenwood, where the thatched roofs hugged the hills and the scent of blooming wildflowers filled the air, life was simple and predictable. The villagers rose with the sun, tended their fields, and gathered in the square to share stories under the twilight sky. Among them was a curious woman named Mira, known for her insatiable thirst for adventure and a heart that longed for something beyond the horizon.

One misty morning, while wandering through a meadow on the outskirts of the village, Mira stumbled upon a peculiar sight. Nestled among the wildflowers stood a shimmering doorway, its frame crafted from intertwining vines and blossoms that pulsed with an ethereal glow. The door itself was adorned with intricate carvings that seemed to shift and dance, reflecting the colors of the meadow. It stood ajar, inviting and mysterious.

Mira approached cautiously, her heart racing with excitement. She had heard whispers of such doorways—legendary portals to other worlds—but had always dismissed them as mere tales. Curiosity overwhelmed her caution. With a deep breath, she pushed the door open and stepped through.

The moment she crossed the threshold, a kaleidoscope of colors enveloped her, swirling and shifting until she landed softly on the ground. Mira looked around, stunned by the vibrant landscape before her. A sprawling forest of luminescent trees stretched into the distance, their leaves shimmering in hues of purple and blue. Strange creatures flitted through the air, their wings like delicate stained glass.

"Welcome to Thaloria," a melodious voice chimed. Mira turned to see a tall figure with pointed ears and iridescent skin standing nearby. The being smiled warmly. "I am Lysander, a guardian of this realm."

"I... I'm Mira," she stammered, her eyes wide with wonder. "I didn't know such a place existed!"

Lysander chuckled, a sound like wind chimes in the breeze. "Many are unaware of the worlds that exist parallel to their own. You were drawn here for a reason, Mira. Thaloria is in need of your spirit."

Mira's heart swelled with purpose. "What can I do?"

"There is a darkness creeping through our lands, threatening to consume the light," Lysander explained, their expression growing somber. "Only a heart untainted by fear can confront it. You possess that heart."

Without hesitation, Mira agreed to help. Guided by Lysander, she journeyed through Thaloria, witnessing its breathtaking beauty and the growing shadows that loomed over its inhabitants. They encountered creatures of all kinds—majestic griffins soaring overhead, mischievous sprites darting between trees, and ancient beings of wisdom who shared stories of the light that once filled the realm.

As they ventured deeper into the heart of Thaloria, they reached the edge of a dark forest known as the Gloomwood. "This is where the darkness resides," Lysander warned. "We must tread carefully."

Mira felt a shiver of apprehension but steeled herself. "Let's go."

As they stepped into the Gloomwood, the air grew heavy, and the vibrant colors faded into shades of gray. Shadows twisted around them, whispering fears and doubts. "You cannot defeat the darkness," they hissed, echoing in her mind. "You are just a mere mortal."

"Do not listen!" Lysander urged. "Stay focused on the light within you."

With every step, the darkness pressed closer, trying to engulf her spirit. Mira felt her resolve wavering. But then, she remembered the warmth of the sun back in Eldenwood, the laughter of her friends, and the beauty of life that had always surrounded her. Gathering her courage, she raised her voice, declaring, "I will not succumb to fear!"

As if responding to her defiance, a brilliant light erupted from within her, illuminating the Gloomwood. The shadows shrieked and recoiled, revealing a path toward a towering obsidian structure at the heart of the darkness.

"There it is," Lysander said, awe in their voice. "The source of the darkness."

With newfound strength, Mira pressed forward, the light guiding her way. Inside the structure, she found a swirling mass of shadows, an entity formed from the fears of those who had lost their hope. It writhed and twisted, a tangible representation of despair.

"Leave this place!" the darkness roared. "You cannot defeat me!"

Mira stood her ground, the warmth of her light enveloping her. "You thrive on fear, but I will not give you that power!"

Drawing upon her memories of love, friendship, and hope, she focused her light toward the dark mass. The shadows hissed, trying to claw their way back, but Mira's determination held firm. "You cannot take my heart! I choose to shine!"

As her light collided with the darkness, a blinding explosion erupted, filling the chamber with radiant energy. The shadows dissipated, their whispers silenced, and in their place, a soft glow emerged, bathing the room in warmth.

In the aftermath, Mira fell to her knees, exhausted but triumphant. The Gloomwood began to change, the gray fading into vibrant colors as life returned. Lysander approached her, eyes filled with gratitude. "You have done it, Mira! You've brought back the light!"

As the sun began to set in Thaloria, Mira realized the truth of her journey. The darkness had not only been a force to battle but a reflection of the fears that dwell within. She had faced those fears and emerged stronger, embracing the light that had always existed in her heart.

With the darkness vanquished, Mira returned to the portal, the glowing amulet still warm against her chest. As she stepped back into the meadow, she felt a shift within her. The experiences in Thaloria had transformed her, igniting a purpose she had never known.

From that day forward, Mira became a guardian of her own world, using her knowledge and strength to inspire others. She shared the tales of Thaloria, encouraging those around her to confront their fears and embrace the light within.

And as the sun set over Eldenwood, casting a golden hue over the village, Mira knew that she had found not just an adventure, but a calling—a reminder that true strength lies in the courage to face the darkness, for it is in that very act that the light shines brightest.

The Heart of the Guardian

In the realm of Lysoria, where mountains kissed the clouds and ancient forests whispered secrets, there existed a powerful artifact known as the Heart of the Guardian. This radiant gem, imbued with the essence of the land itself, protected Lysoria from dark forces and maintained the balance of magic. For centuries, it lay safely within the Temple of Aeloria, guarded by the benevolent priestess, Lyra.

One fateful day, disaster struck. The Heart was stolen by a cunning sorcerer named Malakar, who sought to wield its power for his own malevolent purposes. With the artifact in his possession, the balance of the realm began to crumble, and darkness spread like a disease across the land. Crops withered, rivers ran dry, and despair settled in the hearts of the people.

Among those affected was a young blacksmith named Kaelan, whose forge had become a place of sorrow. With each strike of his hammer, he felt the weight of the darkness pressing down on him. The villagers depended on him, but without the Heart, hope seemed lost. Determined to reclaim the stolen gem, Kaelan made a bold decision. "I will journey to Malakar's lair and bring back the Heart," he declared, his voice resolute.

The townsfolk exchanged glances, a mix of admiration and concern. "You're brave, Kaelan," said Elira, a childhood friend who had always believed in him. "But Malakar is powerful. You need help."

"I will not ask anyone to follow me into danger," he replied, his expression firm. "This is my responsibility."

With a heart full of determination, Kaelan set off at dawn, armed with little more than his blacksmith tools, a dagger, and the strength of his resolve. The path to Malakar's lair led him through the Whispering Woods, a place known for its treacherous terrain and lurking beasts. As he ventured deeper into the forest, the shadows grew thicker, and the air crackled with magic.

As night fell, Kaelan camped beneath the ancient trees, their gnarled roots twisting like serpents. He closed his eyes, hoping for clarity in his dreams. Instead, he was awakened by a rustling sound. Startled, he reached for his dagger, only to find a small creature standing before him—a sprightly fae with shimmering wings.

"Are you lost, brave blacksmith?" the fae asked, her voice like the tinkling of bells.

"I seek the Heart of the Guardian," Kaelan replied, still on edge. "Have you seen it?"

The fae's expression turned serious. "Malakar's fortress lies beyond the woods, guarded by illusions and traps. If you wish to reclaim the Heart, you will need my help."

Reluctantly, Kaelan nodded. "What can you do?"

"I can guide you through the illusions," she said, her wings fluttering excitedly. "But you must promise to listen and trust me."

After a moment's hesitation, Kaelan agreed, and together they set off towards the fortress. As they approached the imposing stone walls, Kaelan felt a shiver run down his spine. The fortress loomed above him, dark and foreboding.

With a flick of her wrist, the fae created a shimmering path through the illusions, leading Kaelan safely past the guards and traps. They slipped through the gates and into the heart of the fortress, where the air was thick with tension.

At the center of the chamber, Kaelan spotted Malakar, the Heart of the Guardian glowing ominously in his grasp. The sorcerer was chanting incantations, dark energy swirling around him. "With this power, I shall bend the realm to my will!" he cackled.

Kaelan's blood boiled at the sight. "Stop!" he shouted, stepping forward. The sorcerer turned, surprised by the intrusion.

"Foolish boy! You think you can challenge me?" Malakar's voice dripped with disdain.

In that moment, the fae whispered, "Distract him! I'll create an opening."

Kaelan nodded, heart racing. He launched himself at Malakar, drawing his dagger and using all his training as a blacksmith to his advantage. "You don't understand the power you toy with!" he yelled, feigning confidence as he dodged the sorcerer's dark magic.

Malakar laughed, casting a spell that sent a wave of shadowy energy toward him. Just then, the fae unleashed her own magic, weaving a protective shield around Kaelan, allowing him to break through the sorcerer's defenses.

"Now!" the fae urged, her voice a chorus of power. Kaelan lunged, grabbing the Heart of the Guardian from Malakar's grasp.

The moment he touched the gem, a blinding light erupted, enveloping him and the fae. The dark magic dissipated, and Malakar staggered back, fury etched on his face. "No! You cannot take it!"

With the Heart in hand, Kaelan felt a surge of strength and clarity wash over him. "This belongs to the people of Lysoria, not to you!"

In that instant, he understood the true power of the Heart was not just in its magic but in its connection to the realm and its people. Channeling this realization, he focused on the Heart, summoning its light.

"By the power of the Guardian, I reclaim what is rightfully ours!" he declared.

A brilliant beam of light shot forth, striking Malakar and engulfing him in a radiant glow. The sorcerer screamed, the darkness within him purging as he vanished, leaving behind only echoes of his rage.

As the chamber quieted, Kaelan felt the warmth of the Heart's energy enveloping him. The fae danced around him, her laughter a melody of triumph. "You did it, brave one!"

Kaelan smiled, holding the Heart high. "We did it together. This belongs to all of us."

Returning to Eldoria, Kaelan was greeted as a hero. The Heart was placed back in its rightful place within the Temple of Aeloria, restoring balance and magic to the realm.

But as the celebrations began, Kaelan felt a familiar tug in his heart. He had started as an orphan, searching for belonging, and now he had found it not only within himself but also within the bonds he had forged along the way. The journey had taught him that true strength lies not in power but in unity and love.

As the stars twinkled overhead, Kaelan realized that while he had reclaimed an artifact of immense power, he had also discovered the greatest treasure of all: the strength that comes from connection and the courage to stand for what is right. And with that knowledge, he felt ready to face whatever the future held.

The Island of Lost Dreams

Captain Elara Stormrider was a figure of legend among the sailors of the Sapphire Sea. Her ship, the *Tempest's Fury*, cut through waves like a blade, its sails billowing against the backdrop of a sunlit horizon. With wild hair and a fierce glint in her eye, Elara was driven by tales of adventure and the search for the legendary island of Eldoria, a mythical place said to appear only once every century.

According to lore, Eldoria was a paradise of unimaginable beauty, filled with treasures beyond reckoning, but it was also a land that tested the hearts and minds of those who dared to seek it. The last sighting of the island had been a hundred years ago, and many had perished trying to find it.

Elara had grown up listening to the stories of her grandfather, a sailor who swore he had glimpsed Eldoria's shores through a veil of mist. "It calls to those with the courage to chase their dreams," he would say, his voice tinged with nostalgia. "But be warned, child, for it can also reveal the truth of your heart."

As the centennial moment approached, Elara gathered her crew—a band of misfits and dreamers, each carrying their own stories and aspirations. They set sail under a brilliant sunset, the promise of adventure igniting their spirits.

Weeks passed as they navigated the tempestuous seas. On the night of the full moon, as the stars aligned in a dazzling array, Elara felt an inexplicable pull, as if the sea itself was whispering secrets to her. "Prepare for course adjustment!" she shouted, the wind rushing through her hair. The crew worked swiftly, eager to follow their captain's instincts.

As they sailed through the dark waters, the ocean began to shimmer, phosphorescent waves illuminating the path ahead. A mist rolled in, swirling around them like a living entity, and just as they thought it would swallow them whole, a landmass emerged from the fog—lush, green, and impossibly beautiful.

"We found it!" Elara cried, exhilaration coursing through her veins. They anchored the ship and prepared to explore the island.

As they stepped ashore, the air was thick with the scent of exotic flowers, and the sound of birdsong filled the air. The crew marveled at the vibrant colors and the otherworldly beauty surrounding them. "This place is a dream," whispered Marek, the ship's navigator, his eyes wide with wonder.

But as they ventured deeper into the island, a sense of unease crept over Elara. The beauty of Eldoria was matched only by its stillness. The vibrant flora thrived, yet the landscape felt eerily deserted. It was as if they had entered a realm frozen in time, untouched by human hands.

Suddenly, they stumbled upon a clearing where towering trees encircled a shimmering pool of water. At its center floated a magnificent, luminescent pearl, pulsating with light. "Look!" Elara exclaimed, her heart racing. "That must be the treasure!"

As she stepped closer, a voice echoed through the clearing, reverberating with wisdom and warmth. "To claim the pearl, you must first confront your deepest desires and fears."

Elara's breath caught in her throat. The voice belonged to a spirit, a guardian of the island. "What do you seek, Captain Stormrider? Riches? Power? Or perhaps something more profound?"

Elara hesitated, her mind racing. She had spent her life chasing adventure, seeking the thrill of the unknown. "I seek the thrill of discovery, the chance to leave my mark on the world!" she declared, but uncertainty lingered in her heart.

The spirit smiled, and the waters of the pool began to swirl, revealing visions of her life—her childhood, the faces of her crew, the longing for connection she often brushed aside in her quest for greatness. "Look deeper, Elara. What truly drives you?"

Suddenly, she saw a vision of herself alone on the sea, her ship empty, the laughter of her crew replaced by haunting silence. It was a future devoid of love and camaraderie, a lonely legacy.

Tears stung her eyes as the realization dawned upon her. "I don't just want to be a great captain. I want to create a home for those I care about. I want to be remembered for the bonds I forged, not just the adventures I chased."

With that confession, the pearl pulsed brighter, resonating with her truth. The spirit nodded, a glimmer of approval in its eyes. "You have discovered the true treasure of Eldoria: the understanding that the journey is not solely about glory but about the connections we make along the way."

As Elara reached for the pearl, the world around her shifted, and she found herself back on the beach, the shimmering pearl resting in her palm. The mist that had once obscured the island began to dissolve, revealing the magnificent landscapes they had explored.

With the pearl in hand, Elara returned to the ship, her heart lighter than it had ever been. The crew welcomed her back with cheers, their spirits lifted by the magic of Eldoria.

As they sailed away from the island, Elara realized that the pearl's magic would not only enrich her life but would also serve as a symbol of her newfound understanding. She vowed to share her experiences and the true essence of adventure with her crew, ensuring they all felt the bonds of friendship that held them together.

In the end, the pearl became a treasured artifact, a reminder that the greatest journey of all is the one that leads us to our true selves, where the heart's desires and the bonds of friendship intertwine in a tapestry of life. And as Elara navigated the vast ocean, she felt not only like a captain but also like a guardian of the dreams that united them all.

Reflections of Desire

In the heart of a forgotten forest, where twisted trees whispered ancient secrets and the air shimmered with magic, there stood an abandoned manor. Once a vibrant home to the illustrious sorceress, Lyra, the manor now lay in ruins, cloaked in vines and shadows. At its center was a grand hall, its walls lined with mirrors, each reflecting not just the physical but the very essence of the souls who dared to gaze into them.

Lyra had been a formidable sorceress, known for her beauty and power. But in her pursuit of ultimate knowledge, she had crossed a line that led to her downfall. Betrayed by her own hubris, she was imprisoned within the very mirror she had used to explore the realms of magic. For centuries, she watched the world through her reflections, yearning for freedom but unable to escape.

One stormy night, a wandering traveler named Aric stumbled upon the manor. He had heard tales of the sorceress and the enchanted forest, but he had never expected to find the ruins. Drawn by an inexplicable pull, he stepped inside, lightning flashing behind him as he entered the grand hall.

The mirrors glimmered in the dim light, each one beckoning him closer. "What secrets do you hold?" he murmured, his fingers brushing against the surface of the glass. Suddenly, one mirror caught his eye—a stunning reflection of a woman with fiery red hair and piercing emerald eyes.

"Help me," her voice resonated, soft yet powerful. "I am trapped, and only a true heart can set me free."

Aric's breath hitched. "Who are you?"

"I am Lyra, the sorceress of this manor," she replied, her voice tinged with desperation. "Long have I lingered in this prison, my magic bound by the betrayal of those I once trusted. Only a true act of courage can shatter the curse that binds me."

Intrigued and moved by her plight, Aric felt a surge of determination. "What must I do?"

"Your heart must be willing to sacrifice what you cherish most," Lyra explained, her gaze piercing into his soul. "Only then can you wield the power to break the enchantment."

Aric pondered her words, realizing the depth of the challenge. He had traveled far and sacrificed much for his freedom, yet he had never faced a test like this. He took a step back, uncertainty creeping into his heart. "What if I fail?"

"Failure is merely a stepping stone to understanding," Lyra replied, her tone calming. "To find your true strength, you must confront your deepest desires. The choice is yours."

Determined to uncover the truth, Aric gazed into the mirror, seeking guidance from his reflection. Suddenly, visions flooded his mind—dreams of glory, adventures that could lead him to unimaginable wealth and power. But alongside those dreams lay memories of companionship, loyalty, and love—the faces of those who had supported him in his journey.

"I've always sought to prove myself," he admitted, his voice thick with emotion. "But perhaps I've lost sight of what truly matters."

Lyra nodded, her expression softening. "The path to true power lies in understanding your heart. What will you choose?"

Taking a deep breath, Aric spoke from the depths of his soul. "I choose to let go of my selfish desires. I want to help you break this curse and return to your true self."

The mirror pulsed with energy, the glass swirling like a tempest. Aric felt a force pull him forward, and in that moment, he understood that his willingness to sacrifice his ambition for another's freedom was the key to breaking the enchantment. "Lyra, I'm ready."

With a flick of her wrist, Lyra called forth the magic of the manor, intertwining it with Aric's intentions. The mirrors around them shimmered, resonating with the power of their connection. "Hold onto your desire for freedom," she urged, her voice a melody of hope.

As the energy surged, Aric felt his body grow lighter. The mirrors began to crack, light spilling from the fractures like beams of dawn breaking through the night. "Let the truth set you free!" Lyra cried, her voice rising above the storm.

In an explosive burst of light, the mirror shattered, sending shards flying through the air like shooting stars. Aric shielded his eyes, feeling the warmth of Lyra's magic envelop him. When he opened his eyes, he stood before Lyra, no longer imprisoned in the glass.

She was breathtaking, her fiery hair cascading like a waterfall, eyes sparkling with newfound life. "You did it!" she exclaimed, joy radiating from her. "You broke the curse!"

But just as joy filled the air, the remnants of the shattered mirror began to swirl and coalesce, revealing a dark figure—Malachai, the sorcerer who had betrayed Lyra. "Foolish mortals! You think you can undo my spell?"

In that moment, Lyra stepped forward, her voice strong and unwavering. "Your darkness has no hold over us! Together, we will banish you!"

With newfound strength coursing through her, Lyra raised her hands, channeling the magic of the Heart of the Guardian. Aric stood beside her, feeling the power of their connection. They joined forces, their magic entwined, casting out the darkness that threatened to consume them.

As Malachai howled in fury, a blinding light engulfed the chamber, banishing him from the realm forever.

As the light faded, Aric and Lyra stood together, their hearts united in purpose. "Thank you for believing in me," she said, her expression filled with gratitude.

"I couldn't have done it without you," Aric replied, realizing the lesson he had learned. The pursuit of power and glory paled in comparison to the bonds forged through sacrifice and selflessness.

Together, they set forth to restore balance to the realm of Lysoria, not as master and servant but as allies united by their shared journey. And as they stepped into the world beyond the shattered mirror, they understood that true magic lay not in power, but in the courage to choose love over ambition, forging a path toward a brighter future.

The Wishkeeper

In the quaint village of Eldridge, nestled between rolling hills and dense forests, tales of the Wishkeeper circulated among the townsfolk like wildfire. The mythical beast, said to be as old as the mountains themselves, granted wishes to those brave enough to find it. However, whispers of the steep price it demanded kept many at bay. Stories told of fortunes and dreams fulfilled but also of lost souls and broken hearts.

Evelyn, a spirited woman with a heart full of dreams, had heard the stories since childhood. An artist at heart, she longed for inspiration that would elevate her work beyond the mundane. She spent her days painting the vibrant landscapes of Eldridge, but deep down, she yearned for something more—a touch of magic to transform her art into a living, breathing experience.

One evening, under the light of a full moon, Evelyn made up her mind. She would seek out the Wishkeeper. Armed with little more than her determination and a sketchbook filled with dreams, she ventured into the woods, guided by the flickering light of fireflies. The air was thick with anticipation, and every rustle of leaves sent shivers down her spine.

After hours of wandering, Evelyn arrived at a clearing. At its center stood a colossal tree, ancient and gnarled, its roots twisting like serpents. It was here, the stories said, that the Wishkeeper resided. Heart pounding, she approached the tree, her fingers brushing against the bark.

Suddenly, a deep rumble echoed through the clearing, and a great shadow unfurled from behind the tree. A magnificent beast emerged, its scales glimmering like gemstones under the moonlight. It had the body of a lion, the wings of a dragon, and eyes that glowed with an otherworldly light. "Who dares seek the Wishkeeper?" it boomed, its voice resonating like thunder.

"I do," Evelyn replied, forcing herself to meet the creature's gaze. "I seek inspiration. I wish to create art that moves the soul."

The Wishkeeper regarded her with a mix of curiosity and amusement. "Many have sought my gifts, but all must pay the price. Are you willing to accept what comes in return for your wish?"

"I am," she declared, her determination unyielding.

"Very well," the Wishkeeper said, extending a massive claw. "What you seek will be granted, but beware: with every gift comes a burden. What you gain will not come without sacrifice."

Evelyn nodded, her heart racing. "I understand."

With a mighty roar, the Wishkeeper swirled around her, and in an instant, she felt a surge of energy coursing through her veins. Colors danced before her eyes, and images flooded her mind—visions of landscapes and emotions she had never encountered. The beast's magic enveloped her, awakening her deepest creativity.

"Your wish is granted," the Wishkeeper announced, settling back into the shadows. "But remember, every inspiration comes from within. Harness it wisely."

Evelyn returned to the village, the weight of her newfound inspiration overwhelming her senses. She painted feverishly, capturing the essence of life and emotion in her work. Her canvases burst with color, and soon the villagers were captivated by her art. Exhibitions followed, and her name became synonymous with beauty and creativity.

Yet, as time passed, Evelyn began to notice a dark cloud hanging over her success. The more she painted, the more distant she felt from herself. The visions that once flowed so freely began to warp and twist, becoming increasingly chaotic. Each stroke of her brush felt like a battle against an unseen force.

One night, consumed by frustration, she returned to the clearing, seeking the Wishkeeper once more. "What have you done to me?" she cried, her voice echoing through the woods. "I sought inspiration, but now I feel lost!"

The shadows stirred, and the Wishkeeper appeared, its eyes piercing through the darkness. "You wished for a gift, but you did not consider the cost of your desires. The burden of inspiration weighs heavily on those unprepared to wield it."

"What do you mean?" Evelyn demanded, feeling desperation clawing at her heart. "I only wanted to create!"

"True artistry comes from authenticity, not from external magic. You have borrowed inspiration without embracing your own voice," the Wishkeeper replied, a note of compassion in its voice. "To reclaim your true essence, you must confront the shadows within yourself."

In that moment, Evelyn understood. She had chased after the Wishkeeper's power, forgetting the importance of her own journey. "What must I do?" she asked, humbled.

"Create from the depths of your heart, not from the gifts of others. Embrace your fears, your failures, and your passions. Only then can you find your true voice," the Wishkeeper instructed.

With newfound clarity, Evelyn returned to her easel, and this time, she painted not for recognition or success, but for herself. She poured her fears, her struggles, and her dreams onto the canvas, allowing her emotions to flow freely.

The colors transformed, each stroke telling a story of resilience and authenticity. As she painted, she felt the weight of the darkness lift, replaced by a profound sense of connection to her art and herself.

Weeks passed, and the villagers marveled at her new work, which radiated a depth of feeling unlike anything they had seen before. But Evelyn no longer painted for their approval; she painted for the joy of creation.

In the end, the Wishkeeper appeared once more, its form glimmering in the moonlight. "You have learned well, Evelyn. The true magic lies within you."

Evelyn smiled, her heart full. "Thank you for showing me the way. I've realized that the greatest inspiration comes from within, not from a gift."

As the Wishkeeper faded into the night, she felt a deep sense of gratitude. The lesson echoed in her heart—a reminder that while desires may lead us to seek external validation, true fulfillment comes from embracing our authentic selves and the journey of self-discovery.

And in that understanding, Evelyn found her voice, creating a legacy that would inspire others long after the last stroke of her brush.

The Canvas of Dreams

In a quaint village nestled between rolling hills, there was a small, unassuming gallery known as *Artisan's Haven*. The gallery was filled with vibrant works from local artists, but one painting, in particular, drew the eye of anyone who entered. It depicted a serene landscape of rolling meadows, a crystal-clear river, and a towering mountain under a starlit sky. It seemed to breathe with life, its colors swirling with an ethereal quality that made it feel almost alive.

The artist, a reclusive woman named Liora, was known for her uncanny ability to capture emotions and moments in her artwork. Despite her talent, Liora rarely displayed her work publicly, preferring to remain in the shadows. Those who dared to inquire about the painting were met with vague answers and a dismissive wave of her hand. Rumors swirled around the village that the painting held secrets far beyond its canvas, but few believed such tales.

One crisp autumn evening, a traveler named Rowan arrived in the village, weary from his journeys. As he entered *Artisan's Haven*, he was immediately captivated by the enchanted painting. Its colors seemed to pulse with an energy that resonated within him, stirring something deep in his soul. "What an extraordinary piece," he murmured, stepping closer to the canvas.

"Ah, the *Whispers of Eldoria*," Liora said softly, appearing from the shadows. Her voice was melodic, and her presence seemed to blend with the painting itself. "It holds the dreams of those who dare to believe."

"Is that so?" Rowan replied, intrigued. "What does it mean?"

"It is said to be a doorway to another realm," Liora replied, a glint of mystery in her eyes. "But it reveals itself only to those who are willing to confront their deepest desires and fears."

Rowan felt an inexplicable connection to the painting, as if it was calling out to him. "Can I enter it?" he asked, a mix of excitement and trepidation coursing through him.

Liora studied him for a moment before nodding. "But remember, what lies beyond may not be what you expect. The realm you seek will reflect your true self, both your light and your shadows."

With determination, Rowan stepped forward, placing his hand on the canvas. The world around him faded, replaced by a whirlwind of colors that enveloped him, pulling him into the depths of the painting.

When he emerged, he found himself standing in the very landscape depicted in the artwork. The air was crisp and fragrant, filled with the scent of blooming flowers and the sound of rushing water. The sky shimmered with an otherworldly glow, casting soft light over the enchanting scene.

In awe, Rowan wandered the meadows, feeling a sense of freedom and joy that had long eluded him. He encountered creatures he had only heard of in tales—graceful deer with antlers of silver, birds that sang melodies of forgotten songs, and gentle fae flitting between flowers.

As he explored, he discovered that the realm held a mirror to his soul. Every joy he felt was amplified, but so too were the shadows he carried. Memories of past failures and fears surfaced, haunting him. "Am I truly worthy of this beauty?" he wondered aloud.

Just then, a figure emerged from the trees—a woman with flowing hair that shimmered like moonlight. "You are not alone in your struggles, Rowan," she said, her voice soft and reassuring. "This realm reveals your heart's truth. Embrace both your light and darkness."

Rowan felt drawn to her, sensing a deep connection. "Who are you?"

"I am Aeliana, the spirit of this realm," she replied. "I guide those who seek to understand themselves. You must confront your fears to unlock the magic of the *Whispers of Eldoria*."

"Can you help me?" he asked, desperation creeping into his voice. "I want to overcome my past."

Aeliana smiled gently. "The power to change lies within you. Face your fears, and the path will reveal itself."

With Aeliana's guidance, Rowan embarked on a journey through the realm, facing manifestations of his doubts and regrets. He climbed the mountain that towered over the landscape, each step symbolizing his struggle to rise above his past. He met visions of himself as a child, filled with dreams, and as a young man, burdened by disappointment.

As he reached the summit, Rowan stood before a mirror that reflected not just his image, but the essence of his journey—the joy of embracing his true self, the pain of letting go, and the strength that had grown from his struggles. "I am more than my failures," he declared, the words resonating with newfound conviction.

In that moment, the mirror shattered, releasing a cascade of light that enveloped him. Rowan felt the weight of his past lift, replaced by a profound sense of peace and acceptance. "I can be whole," he whispered.

As he descended the mountain, the landscape around him began to change. The meadows bloomed brighter, the creatures sang louder, and Aeliana's presence was a guiding light at his side. "You have reclaimed your strength, Rowan," she said, her voice a soothing balm.

With a final burst of energy, they returned to the starting point where he had entered the realm. The enchanted painting shimmered before him, a gateway back to the village. As he stepped through, the world around him blurred and shifted, and he found himself back in *Artisan's Haven*.

Liora stood before him, her eyes reflecting a mixture of pride and understanding. "What did you discover?" she asked.

"I found my truth," Rowan replied, a smile breaking across his face. "I learned that my past does not define me. I can create a new path, filled with hope and authenticity."

Liora nodded, the corners of her mouth lifting in a knowing smile. "You've embraced the lesson of the *Whispers of Eldoria*. True power comes from within, and the courage to face your fears allows you to shape your destiny."

As Rowan left the gallery, he felt lighter, as though he had shed the burdens that had weighed him down for so long. The journey through the enchanted painting had transformed him, granting him not only insight but a renewed sense of purpose.

In the days that followed, he poured his heart into his art, creating pieces that resonated with truth and emotion. The village marveled at his work, but it was not the praise that fueled him; it was the joy of self-expression and the understanding that he had the power to create his own narrative.

And in that realization, Rowan found a piece of the magic he had sought all along—the understanding that true fulfillment comes from embracing one's journey, with all its light and shadows.

Whispers of the Forgotten

In the quaint town of Elden Hollow, where cobblestone streets wound their way past ivy-clad cottages, lived a young boy named Oliver. With tousled hair and a heart full of curiosity, he spent his days exploring the hidden corners of the town, collecting stories from the townsfolk about its rich history and lingering legends. But the tale that intrigued him most was that of the old Whitmore Estate, a crumbling mansion perched on the outskirts of town, rumored to be haunted by the ghost of Lady Eleanor Whitmore.

According to local lore, Lady Eleanor had been a kind and gentle soul who had mysteriously vanished over a century ago, leaving her estate abandoned and shrouded in mystery. Many claimed to have seen her specter wandering the halls, searching for something lost. As Halloween approached, Oliver's curiosity grew, and he decided it was time to uncover the truth about Lady Eleanor and her estate.

One foggy afternoon, armed with nothing but a flashlight and a sense of adventure, Oliver made his way to the Whitmore Estate. The mansion loomed before him, its tall spires piercing the misty sky. Heart pounding with excitement and fear, he pushed open the creaky gate and stepped onto the overgrown path leading to the front door.

The moment he entered, he was enveloped by the scent of dust and decay. Shadows danced along the walls, and the air felt thick with forgotten memories. Oliver explored the dimly lit rooms, taking in the remnants of a bygone era—faded portraits, ornate furniture draped in sheets, and the echoes of laughter long silenced.

As he ventured deeper into the mansion, he heard a soft whisper, a sound so faint he almost dismissed it. "Help me..." the voice sighed, trailing off like a gentle breeze. He paused, his heart racing, and called out, "Is anyone there?"

Suddenly, a figure appeared before him—a translucent woman clad in a flowing gown, her features soft yet tinged with sadness. "I am Lady Eleanor," she said, her voice melodic yet haunting. "I've been trapped in this place for so long."

Oliver's eyes widened in disbelief. "You're real! I thought you were just a story."

"I am both," she replied, a wistful smile gracing her lips. "And I need your help to solve the mystery of my disappearance. Only then can I find peace."

Intrigued, Oliver nodded eagerly. "What do you need me to do?"

"I believe my disappearance is tied to an ancient family heirloom—a locket that holds the key to my past," she explained, her form flickering slightly. "It is hidden somewhere in this house, and I need you to find it."

Determined to help, Oliver began searching the mansion, guided by Lady Eleanor's whispers. They scoured dusty attics filled with cobwebs and shadowy corners that held secrets of the past. With each room they explored, Oliver learned more about Eleanor's life—her kindness, her love for the townsfolk, and the mystery surrounding her family.

As night fell, Oliver felt a growing connection to the ghost. She shared stories of her life, her hopes, and her dreams, and he realized that her spirit was not just bound to the house but to the very fabric of Elden Hollow itself. "Why do you think you disappeared?" he asked, pausing in the middle of a dusty library.

"Some say it was my family's enemies who sought to silence me," Eleanor replied, her eyes shimmering with emotion. "But I believe it was my own inability to confront the darkness that surrounded us."

With a sudden burst of inspiration, Oliver rushed to the attic, where he had spotted an ornate trunk covered in dust. He pried it open, revealing a collection of trinkets and old letters. Among them lay a delicate silver locket, intricately engraved with the Whitmore crest.

"I found it!" Oliver exclaimed, holding up the locket triumphantly.

As he opened it, a warm light enveloped them both. Inside the locket was a faded portrait of a young Eleanor, smiling alongside a man Oliver recognized from the portraits in the hallway. "This is my brother," she murmured, her voice tinged with sorrow. "He was the last person I saw before I vanished."

A wave of emotion washed over Eleanor as the memories flooded back. "He... he was searching for a way to protect me from our enemies. I was too afraid to confront our family's dark legacy. My fear trapped me in this place."

With a flicker of light, the locket glowed brighter, illuminating the room. "I see now," she whispered. "I let fear control me, and in doing so, I lost everything."

As the locket pulsed with energy, Oliver felt the weight of her revelation. "You're not just a ghost. You're a part of the history of this town. By facing your past, you can free yourself and inspire others to confront their fears too."

The light from the locket grew blinding, and Oliver shielded his eyes. When he opened them again, the attic was filled with warmth and color, and Eleanor stood before him, no longer a ghost but a radiant figure of light. "Thank you, dear child," she said, her voice like music. "You have given me the strength to confront my past."

With that, the light enveloped Eleanor, and in an explosion of brilliance, she vanished, leaving behind a sense of peace that filled the room. The locket fell gently to the floor, now a simple silver charm.

As Oliver emerged from the mansion, he felt a profound sense of purpose. He had helped free a lost soul, and in doing so, he had uncovered the importance of facing one's fears. The townsfolk of Elden Hollow would tell stories of Lady Eleanor, not as a ghost but as a guardian spirit who had once walked among them, a reminder that the shadows of the past can be confronted and transformed into light.

In the weeks that followed, Oliver took it upon himself to share Eleanor's story, inspiring others to face their own fears and burdens. He understood now that the greatest legacy one could leave behind was not just a memory, but the courage to confront the darkness, allowing the light to shine through. And in that understanding, he found a purpose greater than he ever imagined.

The Arcane Brotherhood

In the heart of the bustling city of Eldoria, hidden from the prying eyes of the mundane world, lay a clandestine society known as the Arcane Brotherhood. Comprised of powerful magicians, this secretive group was sworn to protect the realm from dark forces that sought to unleash chaos and despair. Their headquarters, an ancient stone tower covered in creeping vines, pulsed with magic and mystery.

Among the Brotherhood was a young sorceress named Elara, known for her sharp mind and unwavering resolve. Despite her impressive abilities, she often felt overshadowed by the more seasoned members of the society. With her long auburn hair and emerald-green robes, she spent her days studying the ancient tomes of magic and honing her skills, dreaming of the day she would prove her worth.

One stormy evening, as lightning illuminated the night sky, the Brotherhood convened for an urgent meeting. The High Mage, an imposing figure with a flowing silver beard, addressed the gathered members. "Darkness stirs in the east," he declared, his voice echoing in the chamber. "A malevolent force known as the Shadow Wyrm threatens to break the barriers between our world and the realm of nightmares. We must act swiftly to stop it."

Elara's heart raced. The Shadow Wyrm was a legendary creature, capable of consuming the very essence of magic. If it were to rise, it could plunge the world into eternal darkness. Determined to contribute, Elara raised her hand. "I can help! Let me assist in the search for the Wyrm's lair."

The other members exchanged glances, some with skepticism, but the High Mage nodded. "Very well, Elara. You may join the expedition. But remember, the darkness is cunning, and it will test your resolve."

With a sense of purpose, Elara gathered her enchanted gear—a staff imbued with protective runes and a satchel filled with potion vials. She set off with a small group of seasoned magicians, including Lucian, a brooding but skilled wizard who had earned his place in the Brotherhood through countless battles against dark forces.

The journey took them through treacherous terrain—twisting forests and craggy mountains, where shadows danced among the trees. Elara focused on harnessing her magic, weaving spells to protect and guide them. But despite her determination, self-doubt crept in. Would she be able to match the prowess of her companions?

As they ventured deeper into the wilderness, they stumbled upon a desolate village, its buildings crumbling and overgrown with vines. The air was heavy with despair, and a chilling wind whispered through the empty streets. "This place feels cursed," Elara murmured.

Lucian nodded, his expression serious. "The Shadow Wyrm feeds on fear and sorrow. It leaves ruin in its wake."

Just then, a flicker of movement caught Elara's eye. A young girl stood among the ruins, her wide eyes filled with terror. "Please, help us!" she cried, her voice trembling. "The darkness is coming!"

Elara felt a surge of compassion. "We will help you. Where is the darkness?"

The girl pointed toward a shadowy figure lurking at the edge of the village, tendrils of darkness swirling around it like smoke. Elara's heart sank—this was no mere manifestation of fear but a servant of the Shadow Wyrm itself.

"Stand together!" Lucian commanded, raising his staff. The group formed a protective circle around the girl, readying their spells. As the creature advanced, Elara felt her magic rising within her. She closed her eyes and focused, channeling her energy into a barrier of light.

With a blinding flash, the magic erupted, illuminating the village. The creature recoiled, hissing and writhing as it was pushed back. But Elara sensed the strain on her energy; the darkness was formidable, and the confrontation was taking its toll.

"Keep it at bay!" Lucian shouted, casting powerful spells to fend off the creature. The battle raged, spells flying through the air, illuminating the night like fireworks. Elara pushed herself harder, the light from her barrier flickering dangerously.

In a moment of clarity, she understood that the source of the darkness was not just the creature but the collective fear of the villagers. Drawing on her compassion, Elara reached out to the young girl. "What is your name?"

"Lina," the girl whispered, her voice barely audible over the chaos.

"Lina, focus on the light!" Elara urged. "We need your strength! Picture something beautiful, something that makes you feel safe."

The girl nodded, her expression shifting from fear to determination. She closed her eyes and concentrated. Elara could feel a shift in the energy around them as the light from her barrier began to swell, fed by the warmth of hope.

With a renewed sense of purpose, Elara directed her energy toward Lina, merging their magic. "Together!" she called out, feeling the strength of the girl's belief bolster her own. The barrier exploded with light, a brilliant beacon that pierced through the darkness, illuminating the village and banishing the creature back into the shadows.

As the creature dissipated, the oppressive atmosphere lifted, and the village began to glow with newfound vitality. Lina opened her eyes, her face radiant. "You did it! We did it!" she exclaimed.

Elara's heart swelled with joy, but as the light faded, she felt a sense of uncertainty. "What now?" she asked, looking at Lucian and the others.

"You've shown us the true power of magic," Lucian said, a proud smile on his face. "It's not just about strength; it's about hope and connection. You've proven that even in darkness, light can emerge when we come together."

As the group prepared to leave the village, Elara felt a sense of fulfillment. They had faced the darkness not just with spells but with compassion and unity. The experience had transformed her, instilling a deep understanding that true power lay in the bonds forged through shared struggles.

With the villagers behind her, Elara led the way back to the Brotherhood, the fire of purpose burning brightly within her. She had learned that magic was not merely an art to wield, but a force to nurture and share. And as they stepped into the dawn of a new day, she understood that the journey against the darkness was not just one of battle, but a quest for the light that lived in every heart.

The Elemental Trials

In the majestic kingdom of Aetheria, where mountains kissed the sky and rivers sparkled like diamonds, the annual Elemental Trials were the highlight of the year. This magical tournament drew competitors from all corners of the realm, each vying for the coveted title of Elemental Champion. The victor would gain mastery over the four elements—earth, water, fire, and air—and wield the power to shape the world itself.

Among the competitors was Kaelan, a young mage with a fiery spirit and a determination to prove himself. With tousled hair and a heart full of dreams, he had trained for this moment his entire life. The whispers of his lineage, the last descendant of a forgotten line of powerful elemental mages, echoed in his mind as he prepared for the trials.

The tournament took place in a grand arena, surrounded by ancient stone walls and vibrant banners that fluttered in the breeze. The crowd buzzed with excitement as the competitors took their places, each representing their elemental affinity. Kaelan stood with the other fire mages, his heart pounding as the High Mage, an imposing figure draped in robes of all colors, stepped forward to announce the start of the trials.

"Welcome, seekers of power! The Elemental Trials shall begin!" he boomed, his voice resonating throughout the arena. "May the best mage rise to claim mastery over the elements!"

The first challenge involved the competitors harnessing their elemental powers to create a stunning display. Kaelan focused, summoning flames that danced and twirled in intricate patterns, eliciting gasps of awe from the crowd. But as the fire blazed higher, he felt the pressure to perform, and a flicker of doubt crept in.

After a series of challenges testing their strength, wit, and control over their elements, Kaelan found himself in the final round. Only three competitors remained: him, a graceful water mage named Lira, and a brooding earth mage named Garrick. The atmosphere crackled with tension as they prepared for the ultimate showdown.

The High Mage stepped forward, his eyes gleaming with anticipation. "The final challenge will determine the fate of the elements themselves. You will face each other in an elemental clash, where only the strongest will prevail."

As the three competitors took their positions, Kaelan felt a surge of energy coursing through him. This was it. This was his moment to prove himself. The High Mage raised his staff, and a wave of magical energy enveloped the arena, signaling the start of the battle.

The clash began, and the arena transformed into a chaotic tapestry of elemental fury. Lira summoned torrents of water that crashed against Kaelan's flames, while Garrick commanded the earth to rise up, creating barriers and obstacles. The ground shook with the force of their magic, and Kaelan found himself caught in a whirlwind of power.

Determined to seize control, he focused on the fire within him, letting it ignite his spirit. With a fierce shout, he unleashed a wave of flames, pushing back against Lira's water and shattering Garrick's stone walls. The arena erupted in cheers, and for a moment, Kaelan felt invincible.

But just as victory seemed within reach, the elemental forces collided in a devastating explosion, sending shockwaves rippling through the arena. As the dust settled, Kaelan found himself disoriented and alone, the other competitors seemingly vanished.

"Where are they?" he wondered aloud, his heart racing. Panic began to seep in as he realized he was no longer in the arena but in a desolate landscape, a barren wasteland of cracked earth and swirling winds.

"Welcome to the Realm of the Elements," a voice echoed around him. Kaelan turned to see a figure materialize from the shadows—a tall woman with flowing robes adorned with elemental symbols. "I am Aeloria, the Guardian of the Elements. You have been summoned to face the truth of your heart."

Kaelan's confusion deepened. "What do you mean? I came to compete!"

Aeloria shook her head, her eyes filled with understanding. "The trials test not just your magic but your intentions. The true mastery of the elements lies in understanding their balance, not in dominating them."

"What do you mean?" he asked, frustration boiling within him. "I want to be the champion! I want the power to change the world!"

"Power without understanding leads to destruction," Aeloria replied, her voice calm yet firm. "You must confront the truth of your desires and the cost of ambition."

As she spoke, Kaelan felt visions flash before him—scenes of power wielded recklessly, firestorms consuming villages, floods overwhelming cities, and mountains collapsing under the weight of greed. The realization hit him like a tidal wave: he had focused solely on victory, blind to the consequences of unchecked ambition.

"You sought power, but true strength lies in harmony," Aeloria said, her voice guiding him through his turmoil. "Can you find balance within yourself?"

Kaelan closed his eyes, reflecting on his journey—the people he had met, the friendships he had forged, and the lessons he had learned. He understood now that the elements were not just tools to wield but living forces that required respect and understanding.

With newfound clarity, he opened his eyes. "I want to protect the balance, to use my power to bring harmony to the world. I will not let my ambition blind me again."

Aeloria smiled, the landscape shifting around them as she gestured toward the horizon. "Your heart has found its truth. You may return to the arena, but remember: the greatest mastery comes not from dominating the elements, but from embracing their unity."

With a wave of her hand, the world dissolved, and Kaelan found himself back in the arena, the crowd cheering as he stood victorious over Lira and Garrick. But as the High Mage declared him the champion, Kaelan raised his hands to silence them.

"I cannot accept this title without acknowledging the truth of our journey," he proclaimed, his voice echoing through the arena. "We must unite our powers, not dominate them. Together, we can protect the balance of our world."

The crowd fell silent, then erupted into applause, and Lira and Garrick joined him, understanding the message he had shared. Together, they vowed to protect Eldoria from any darkness that threatened to disrupt the harmony of the elements.

And so, the Elemental Trials became a testament to the strength found in unity, reminding all who heard the tale that true power lies not in ambition, but in the wisdom to understand and respect the forces that shape their world.

The Healer of Aeloria

In the ancient kingdom of Aeloria, where lush forests met sprawling meadows, tales of a legendary healer known as Sylas circulated among the townsfolk like a gentle breeze. This healer was said to possess the extraordinary ability to cure any ailment—physical or otherwise. For those suffering from dire illnesses, Sylas was a beacon of hope, a figure wrapped in mystery, residing deep within the Enchanted Woods.

When word reached Elara, a young woman with a heart of gold and a fierce determination, that her ailing mother's condition had worsened, she knew what she had to do. Her mother had always been her guiding light, and Elara couldn't bear the thought of losing her. With a heavy heart and a fierce resolve, she set off on a quest to find Sylas.

The journey began at dawn, the sun casting a golden hue over the fields as Elara packed provisions and set her sights on the distant woods. As she entered the Enchanted Woods, the air thickened with magic, the trees whispering ancient secrets. She had heard stories of the forest's enchantments—how paths shifted and illusions danced in the twilight—but her determination steered her forward.

Days passed as Elara navigated the labyrinthine trails, encountering creatures of wonder and whimsy. She met sprites who played tricks, wise old owls that offered cryptic advice, and a gentle centaur named Arion who agreed to guide her deeper into the woods. "The way to Sylas is fraught with challenges," Arion warned. "Many seek him, but few are truly ready for what lies ahead."

"I am ready," Elara replied firmly. "I will do whatever it takes to save my mother."

As they journeyed together, Arion shared stories of Sylas—how he had once been a revered healer in the kingdom, beloved by all, until a tragic event had driven him into seclusion. "He carries the weight of his past," Arion explained. "It may be the key to understanding his gifts."

When they finally reached Sylas's dwelling, a quaint cottage nestled among ancient oaks, Elara's heart raced. The air crackled with energy, and the scent of herbs filled her senses. She approached the door, but before she could knock, it swung open, revealing a man with silver hair and deep-set eyes that seemed to hold the weight of a thousand stories.

"Why have you come?" Sylas asked, his voice a mixture of weariness and curiosity.

"My mother is gravely ill," Elara implored, desperation filling her voice. "I've traveled far to seek your help. They say you can cure any ailment."

Sylas studied her intently, his gaze piercing. "Many have come seeking healing, but healing is not simply about the body. It involves the heart, the spirit, and the soul. Are you prepared to confront the truth of your mother's ailment?"

"What do you mean?" Elara's confusion deepened.

"Follow me," he said, stepping aside. As she entered the cottage, Elara was enveloped in the scent of dried herbs and the soft glow of candlelight. Sylas gestured for her to sit. "To heal your mother, we must first understand the source of her suffering."

With a wave of his hand, the room transformed, revealing swirling images of Elara's mother—a vibrant woman filled with life. But as the images shifted, they revealed a deeper truth: moments of sadness, loss, and unspoken regrets that had shadowed her heart.

"You see," Sylas said gently, "her ailment is not just physical. It is tied to her emotions, her past. Healing comes from within. We must address the pain she carries."

Elara felt her heart constrict. "But how can I help her with that? I've always relied on others to fix things."

"You must confront your own feelings as well," Sylas advised, his tone encouraging. "Only then can you support her journey to healing."

Determined, Elara closed her eyes and focused on her memories of her mother—the laughter, the love, and the moments of hardship. She had often felt helpless, wishing to ease her mother's burdens but unsure how to approach the deeper issues. "I never wanted to admit that she was suffering," she whispered. "I thought I could protect her."

"You cannot protect her by shielding her from her emotions," Sylas replied. "You must be honest and open. Only through vulnerability can you both find healing."

With a newfound resolve, Elara returned to her village. She embraced her mother, sharing everything—the fears she held about her health, her desire to shield her from pain, and her commitment to be there through the difficult moments. As they spoke, Elara felt the weight lift from her heart, and for the first time, she saw a glimmer of hope in her mother's eyes.

Over the following weeks, they worked together, confronting old wounds and nurturing their bond. Elara learned to communicate openly, to share laughter and tears, and to create a space where healing could flourish.

One evening, as they sat in the garden, a gentle breeze rustling the leaves, Elara's mother took her hand. "Thank you for being brave, my dear," she said, her voice soft yet strong. "I've felt so alone in my struggles, but you've reminded me that we can face them together."

As they embraced, Elara understood that healing was not simply about fixing the body; it was about connection, love, and the willingness to confront the shadows that lurked within. The lessons from Sylas echoed in her heart, guiding her toward a deeper understanding of what it meant to truly heal.

Months later, as her mother regained her strength, Elara returned to the Enchanted Woods, seeking Sylas to thank him for his guidance. When she reached his cottage, she found it empty, yet the air felt alive with magic. On the table lay a note: "Healing begins when we embrace the truth within. Remember, you hold the power to nurture love and healing in your own heart."

With a smile, Elara understood that she would carry Sylas's wisdom with her always, embracing the beauty of vulnerability and the transformative power of love. She had sought a healer, but in doing so, she had discovered the healer within herself.

The Shadow of Aeloria

In the realm of Aeloria, where once the sun shone bright and the laughter of children filled the streets, darkness had crept in, casting a pall over the land. King Alaric, a tyrant consumed by power, wielded dark magic that twisted the hearts of those who served him. The once-flourishing kingdom had fallen into despair, its people oppressed under the weight of fear and cruelty.

In a hidden corner of Aeloria, a rebellion was brewing. Led by a fierce warrior named Kaelin and a cunning sorceress named Mira, a group of brave souls gathered in secrecy to plot the overthrow of their malevolent king. Each had suffered under Alaric's reign: families torn apart, livelihoods destroyed, dreams crushed. United by their pain, they dared to believe in the possibility of freedom.

One stormy night, as lightning illuminated the sky, Kaelin stood at the head of their makeshift table, a map of the castle spread out before him. "We strike at dawn," he declared, his voice steady despite the storm raging outside. "The guards will be at their weakest after the king's nightly rituals. We'll have a chance to infiltrate the castle and confront Alaric before he can summon his dark magic."

Mira, her silver hair reflecting the flickering candlelight, leaned in closer. "But we must be cautious. Alaric has eyes everywhere, and his magic can sense our movements. If we are discovered, it will spell doom for us all."

The rebels nodded, their expressions a mixture of determination and fear. They were aware of the risks, but the thought of living under Alaric's tyranny any longer fueled their resolve. As they prepared for the coming battle, Kaelin felt a flicker of hope in his heart—perhaps today would mark the dawn of a new era for Aeloria.

As the first light of dawn broke, they set their plan into motion. Clad in dark cloaks, they made their way toward the castle, hearts pounding in unison. The air was thick with tension, and the distant sounds of the kingdom awakening only intensified their resolve. They reached the castle gates, their breaths shallow and quick.

Mira raised her hand, casting a spell that cloaked them in shadows, rendering them invisible to the guards. They slipped through the gates and into the dark halls of the castle, where the echoes of their footsteps mingled with the whispers of dread.

As they navigated the twisting corridors, they encountered guards patrolling the halls. With a wave of her hand, Mira cast a spell that lulled them into a deep sleep, allowing the rebels to pass undetected.

Finally, they reached the throne room, its grand doors adorned with intricate carvings depicting Alaric's rise to power. Kaelin pushed open the doors, and they stepped inside, ready to confront the tyrant. The room was dimly lit, shadows flickering along the walls. At the far end, Alaric sat upon his throne, draped in dark robes, his eyes glowing with a sinister light.

"Welcome, rebels," he sneered, his voice a chilling blend of mockery and menace. "Did you truly think you could challenge me? You are fools to believe you could defy the shadows."

Mira stepped forward, determination in her eyes. "Your reign of terror ends today, Alaric. The people of Aeloria will no longer live in fear of your dark magic."

Alaric laughed, a sound that echoed through the chamber like a death knell. "You think you can defeat me with your petty courage? I am power incarnate!"

As he spoke, the shadows in the room swirled and coalesced, forming dark tendrils that lashed out toward the rebels. Kaelin drew his sword, the blade gleaming with the light of their hopes. "Stand together!" he shouted.

The rebels formed a protective circle, their combined magic and courage creating a barrier against the encroaching darkness. Mira channeled her energy, summoning a bright shield that glimmered like starlight, pushing back the tendrils of shadow.

"Feel the weight of your actions, Alaric!" she cried, her voice steady. "You have terrorized this kingdom for too long!"

With a surge of determination, Kaelin charged at the throne, his sword raised high. "Your reign is over!" He swung the blade, aiming for the heart of darkness that fueled the tyrant's power.

But just as the blade was about to connect, a blinding flash erupted from Alaric, sending Kaelin sprawling backward. The king's laughter echoed through the chamber as shadows danced around him. "You're too late, little hero! You see, my power comes from fear itself. As long as there are those who fear me, I shall never fall!"

With that, the shadows surged forward again, threatening to engulf the rebels. Just then, Kaelin remembered something his father had told him long ago. "Fear is a choice. It can only thrive in darkness."

With a fierce resolve, Kaelin stood up, his heart pounding, and looked at his friends. "Remember why we fight! We are stronger together. We choose to stand against him, and that choice will light our way!"

Drawing upon the strength of their unity, the rebels focused their magic together, forming a brilliant sphere of light that radiated hope and courage. As the light surged forward, it clashed with Alaric's shadows, illuminating the room with pure brilliance.

The shadows writhed and recoiled, unable to withstand the force of their combined resolve. Kaelin took the opportunity and charged once more, driving his sword into the heart of the shadows, which shattered like glass.

In an explosion of light, Alaric was thrown back, his figure dissolving into wisps of darkness. "No! This cannot be!" he screamed as his power evaporated, leaving behind nothing but silence.

As the light faded and the dust settled, Kaelin and his friends stood panting in the now peaceful throne room. They had faced their fears and emerged victorious, but as they looked around, they realized that the castle had transformed into a symbol of hope.

Mira turned to the others, her eyes shining with pride. "We did it! Together, we brought down the darkness."

Kaelin smiled, but he understood that the true victory lay not only in defeating Alaric but in the strength they had found within themselves. "We learned that courage can conquer fear, but it's our unity that gives us true power."

With the dawn of a new day breaking outside the castle walls, the rebels stepped into the sunlight, ready to rebuild Aeloria and lead it into a future free from tyranny. They knew that the shadows might return, but armed with the lessons of their journey, they would stand together, stronger than ever before.

The Eternal Flame

In the heart of the fiery mountain range of Pyraxis, where the sky glowed crimson and the earth pulsed with the heat of ancient lava flows, lived a magnificent phoenix named Seraphis. With feathers that shimmered like molten gold and eyes that burned with the essence of the sun, Seraphis was a creature of legend. However, beneath his brilliant exterior lay a heart burdened with a deep yearning for something more—immortality.

Every century, the phoenix underwent a transformative cycle, bursting into flames and rising anew from his ashes. While this rebirth granted him renewed strength, Seraphis was haunted by the fleeting nature of his existence. He had witnessed countless friends and foes perish, their flames extinguished forever. Driven by desperation, he sought the fabled Flame of Immortality, said to be hidden deep within the mystical Firestone Caverns.

"Only by finding the Flame can a phoenix gain true immortality," the elders had whispered, their voices steeped in reverence. "But beware, for the Flame does not come without its price."

Determined, Seraphis set out on his quest, soaring high above the peaks, feeling the heat of the sun on his wings. He navigated treacherous paths and swirling winds, finally arriving at the entrance of the Firestone Caverns. The air crackled with magic, and the walls glowed with fiery crystals, illuminating the darkness ahead.

As he ventured deeper into the cavern, the temperature soared. The passageways twisted and turned, echoing with the sounds of bubbling magma and distant roars. Suddenly, Seraphis found himself face-to-face with a colossal creature—a Fire Drake, its scales glinting like embers in the dark.

"Who dares enter my domain?" the Fire Drake growled, smoke billowing from its nostrils.

"I am Seraphis, the phoenix, and I seek the Flame of Immortality," he declared, his voice unwavering. "I must find it to embrace my true destiny."

The Fire Drake narrowed its eyes, sizing him up. "Many have sought the Flame, yet few are deemed worthy. Tell me, what are you willing to sacrifice for such power?"

Seraphis hesitated, pondering the depths of his desire. "I will sacrifice anything—my treasures, my status, my very essence—if it means gaining true immortality."

The Drake laughed, a sound like crackling fire. "You speak boldly, phoenix, but be warned: immortality comes with burdens. Will you be prepared to carry the weight of eternity?"

Undeterred, Seraphis nodded. "I will bear whatever price necessary."

The Drake gestured for him to follow, leading him through a series of fiery chambers, each filled with breathtaking beauty and unimaginable peril. As they traveled, Seraphis faced challenges that tested his strength and resolve—a trial of flames that required him to confront his deepest fears, a tempest of ash that sought to snuff out his spirit. Each obstacle only strengthened his determination, and the Fire Drake watched with a mix of intrigue and respect.

Finally, they arrived at the Chamber of Flames, a vast room where a towering pyre flickered with brilliant colors. At its core, the Flame of Immortality danced, a swirling vortex of light and heat. Seraphis felt its warmth wash over him, calling to his very essence.

"You have reached the Flame," the Fire Drake rumbled. "Now, make your choice. Touch it, and you will gain immortality, but know that you will lose all memories of your past life—the friends you cherished, the battles you fought, the joys and sorrows that shaped you."

Seraphis stepped closer, the Flame's brilliance intoxicating. He imagined a life free from death, a chance to witness the world evolve through the ages. But as he extended his wing toward the Flame, memories flooded his mind—laughter shared with friends, the warmth of the sun on his feathers, the quiet moments of reflection.

In that instant, clarity struck him. "No," he breathed, withdrawing his wing. "I do not want to forget. My past, with all its pain and beauty, is what makes me who I am. I would rather embrace the cycles of life than live without the memories that shape me."

The Fire Drake looked surprised, and for the first time, a hint of respect gleamed in its eyes. "You have chosen wisely, phoenix. True immortality lies not in the absence of death, but in the richness of experiences that life brings."

As Seraphis turned to leave, the Flame of Immortality flickered, its glow softening. "You will carry your memories with you through each rebirth. Embrace the beauty of life and death, for they are intertwined."

With newfound wisdom, Seraphis soared from the caverns, the heat of the Flame still echoing in his heart. He understood that immortality was not simply about defying death but about cherishing every moment, every relationship, and every lesson learned along the way.

Returning to the sunlit skies of Aeloria, Seraphis embraced his life as it was—full of cycles, joy, and inevitable sorrow. He chose to become a guardian of the memories he held dear, using his experiences to guide others on their paths.

And in that choice, he discovered a deeper magic—the magic of living fully, embracing the ephemeral beauty of life, and knowing that the true essence of existence lay not in eternal life but in the love and connections forged along the way.

The Guardian's Oath

In the tranquil village of Eldenwood, nestled between emerald hills and dense forests, the villagers lived in harmony, guided by the whispers of nature and the watchful eye of their guardian spirit, Aeloria. This ethereal being, a shimmering figure of light and wind, had watched over the village for centuries, protecting it from dark forces that lingered in the shadows. The villagers revered her, offering flowers and prayers, believing her presence kept the ancient evils at bay.

However, peace can often breed complacency. As the years passed, stories of the old world faded into myth, and the villagers began to take Aeloria's protection for granted. They grew careless, ignoring the warnings of the elders who spoke of a time when darkness would rise again.

One fateful evening, a chilling wind swept through Eldenwood, and the air thickened with an ominous energy. The sky turned an unnatural shade of crimson, and whispers of dread echoed through the village. Panic spread as the villagers gathered in the square, fear etched on their faces.

"Something stirs in the darkness," Elder Rowan warned, his voice trembling. "The ancient evil we thought defeated has returned. We must call upon Aeloria to protect us!"

But as they called for their guardian, no shimmering light descended from the skies. The silence was deafening, and the villagers grew uneasy. The last rays of sunlight faded, plunging the village into an eerie twilight.

Amidst the chaos, a young woman named Elowen stepped forward. Fierce and resolute, she had always felt a deep connection to Aeloria, sensing the spirit's presence in the rustling leaves and the gentle breeze. "We cannot wait for Aeloria to save us," she declared. "We must confront the darkness ourselves. If we are to protect our home, we must seek out the source of this evil."

The villagers hesitated, but Elowen's determination sparked a fire within them. They formed a small band, armed with makeshift weapons and torches, and set out into the encroaching darkness, guided by the flickering light of their flames.

As they ventured deeper into the forest, shadows danced between the trees, and the chilling wind whispered ominous secrets. The group pressed on, led by Elowen's unwavering spirit. After hours of searching, they stumbled upon a clearing where the ground was scorched and barren. In the center stood an ancient altar, dark and twisted, pulsating with malevolent energy.

"It's here," Elowen breathed, her heart racing. "This must be the source of the darkness."

Suddenly, the air crackled, and a figure emerged from the shadows—an imposing figure cloaked in darkness, with eyes that glowed like embers. "You dare to trespass in my domain?" it hissed, the voice echoing with malice. "Foolish mortals. Your guardian cannot save you now."

Fear gripped the villagers, but Elowen stood her ground. "We may be foolish, but we will not stand by and let you destroy our home!"

The figure laughed, a sound filled with contempt. "Your bravery is admirable, but it will not save you. Aeloria has abandoned you, and soon, the village will fall to darkness!"

Elowen felt a flicker of doubt, but she quickly remembered the stories of Aeloria's strength and the love the villagers had shown her. "Aeloria may be distant, but her spirit lives in us! We will fight for our home, for the light that remains within us!"

With renewed determination, Elowen raised her torch high, the flames dancing in the night. The villagers joined her, forming a united front against the encroaching darkness. Together, they chanted words of protection learned from their ancestors, invoking the spirit of Aeloria.

As their voices echoed through the clearing, the shadows writhed and recoiled, and a beam of light pierced through the darkness, illuminating the altar. The figure screeched in fury, but Elowen stood firm, her heart pounding with the energy of their combined will.

In that moment, something unexpected happened. The light swirled and coalesced, revealing Aeloria in her full glory. "You have called upon me in your time of need," she proclaimed, her voice resonating like a gentle breeze. "But it is your courage and unity that have brought me back. Together, we shall vanquish this darkness!"

With a wave of her hand, Aeloria unleashed a torrent of light, engulfing the shadowy figure. The darkness twisted and howled, but it could not withstand the combined strength of the villagers' resolve and the spirit of their guardian. In a blinding flash, the figure dissipated, leaving behind only a faint whisper that echoed through the clearing.

As the light faded, the villagers found themselves standing together in the clearing, the air fresh and filled with hope. They had faced the darkness and emerged victorious, but Elowen felt a stirring in her heart. "We must remember this moment," she said, looking around at her friends. "We cannot let ourselves become complacent again. We must honor Aeloria's spirit and protect our home together."

The villagers nodded in agreement, understanding the lesson learned that night. They had called upon Aeloria in their time of need, but it was their unity, their courage, and their willingness to confront the darkness that had ultimately saved them.

As they made their way back to Eldenwood, the dawn broke on the horizon, casting golden rays over the land. The villagers rejoiced, their hearts lightened by the knowledge that they were not alone. They had a guardian spirit watching over them, but more importantly, they had each other.

From that day forward, the village thrived, not just in the presence of their guardian but through the bonds they had forged. They celebrated their victories, learned from their struggles, and vowed to protect one another against the darkness that lurked in the corners of their world.

And in the quiet moments, when the wind rustled through the trees, they could still hear Aeloria's gentle whispers, a reminder of the strength that comes from unity and the light that dwells within each of them.

The Alchemist's Legacy

In the heart of the bustling city of Verenthia, known for its vibrant markets and the scent of spices that danced through the air, there lived an alchemist named Roderick. With wild hair and ink-stained fingers, he spent his days in a cluttered workshop filled with glass vials, bubbling potions, and dusty tomes. Roderick was obsessed with one goal: to create the fabled Philosopher's Stone, the legendary substance that could turn base metals into gold and grant the gift of immortality.

Roderick had devoted years to studying ancient texts and experimenting with various ingredients. The allure of the Philosopher's Stone was not just in its power; it represented the pinnacle of alchemical achievement. "With it, I could change the world!" he often exclaimed to his skeptical assistant, Mira, a sharp-witted young woman with an eye for detail.

"Or you could destroy it," Mira replied dryly, watching Roderick's frantic pace as he mixed a new concoction. "You know the legends warn of the consequences. Many have tried, and few have succeeded."

Roderick waved her off, his mind racing with possibilities. "They were not as skilled as I am! I can feel it in my bones; I'm close!" His obsession blinded him to the dangers surrounding his quest.

One evening, while rummaging through a forgotten chest of books, Roderick stumbled upon a tattered manuscript, its pages filled with cryptic symbols and forgotten lore. Among the intricate drawings was a sketch of the Philosopher's Stone and a passage detailing a rare flower called the Celestia Bloom, which was said to be the key ingredient in its creation. According to the manuscript, the bloom only blossomed once every hundred years atop the treacherous peaks of Mount Verath.

Determined to acquire the flower, Roderick packed his belongings and set off on the perilous journey. He knew that finding the Celestia Bloom was the final step to achieving his dream. Mira, who had little faith in his reckless pursuits, reluctantly decided to follow him, sensing that the journey would be fraught with dangers he had yet to consider.

As they climbed the mountain, the air grew thin, and the landscape became increasingly treacherous. They battled fierce winds and icy trails, pushing forward against nature's wrath. Along the way, they encountered strange creatures and obstacles that tested their resolve. Each challenge reminded Roderick of the power of nature—a force far beyond his alchemical ambitions.

After several grueling days, they finally reached the summit, where the air was crisp and cold. In a small clearing bathed in sunlight, they found the Celestia Bloom, its petals glowing like soft blue flames. Roderick gasped in awe, rushing forward to pluck the flower from its delicate stem.

As he held the bloom, a low rumble echoed through the mountains. Suddenly, a massive figure emerged from the shadows—a guardian spirit of the mountain, with eyes like molten gold and a voice that resonated like thunder. "You dare to take what is sacred without understanding its worth?" the spirit boomed, towering over them.

Roderick's heart raced. "I seek to create the Philosopher's Stone! I have devoted my life to this quest!"

"The stone holds great power," the guardian replied, stepping closer. "But it also carries a heavy burden. Many have pursued its creation, but few have returned. Do you understand what you seek?"

Mira stepped forward, her voice steady. "He seeks knowledge and the chance to change the world, but what will he lose in the process?"

The guardian regarded her thoughtfully. "You both stand at a crossroads. The stone can grant wealth and immortality, but it requires a sacrifice of the heart. Are you prepared to give up what you cherish most?"

Roderick faltered, the weight of the guardian's words sinking in. "I only wish to make a better world," he replied, uncertainty creeping into his voice.

"True change comes not from power but from understanding the value of life itself," the guardian said. "The stone can give you what you desire, but it cannot grant you wisdom or compassion."

The realization struck Roderick like a lightning bolt. He had been so consumed by his ambition that he had overlooked the true essence of alchemy: the transformation of the self. In that moment, he understood that the pursuit of the Philosopher's Stone had blinded him to the importance of the journey, the relationships he had forged, and the knowledge he had gained.

"I...I cannot take it," Roderick said, his voice trembling. "Not if it means sacrificing what truly matters."

The guardian smiled, a warm light radiating from its form. "You have chosen wisely, alchemist. True mastery lies not in the acquisition of power but in the wisdom to recognize what is truly valuable."

As Roderick placed the Celestia Bloom back on its stem, the mountain sighed with relief. The guardian faded back into the shadows, leaving them with a sense of peace.

On their descent, Roderick and Mira reflected on their journey. They had faced danger and uncertainty, but in doing so, they discovered the essence of their own hearts. The pursuit of power paled in comparison to the strength found in understanding and compassion.

Back in Eldenwood, Roderick transformed his workshop into a place of learning, sharing his knowledge of alchemy with the villagers. He taught them that true alchemy was not just about transforming substances but also about transforming lives.

And as the years passed, Roderick found fulfillment not in the Philosopher's Stone but in the connections he forged and the wisdom he imparted. He realized that the greatest treasures in life could not be created or obtained but were the lessons learned along the way—the heart's true legacy.

The Land of Giants

In the sleepy town of Millbrook, where the streets were lined with quaint cottages and the scent of fresh-baked bread wafted through the air, a group of friends—Sam, Mia, Jake, and Lila—often found themselves seeking adventure. They were in their late twenties, bound by years of friendship, and united by their shared desire to escape the monotony of daily life.

One weekend, as they ventured into the woods on the outskirts of town, they stumbled upon a curious sight: a large, gnarled tree with roots twisting above the ground, forming an archway. "This looks like something out of a fairy tale," Mia remarked, her eyes sparkling with excitement.

"Only one way to find out," Jake replied, stepping forward with an adventurous grin. The others exchanged glances, a mix of excitement and trepidation, before following him through the archway.

As they passed beneath the roots, a strange shimmering light enveloped them, and suddenly, they found themselves in an entirely different world. The air was thick with magic, and towering trees stretched high above, their leaves glimmering like emeralds in the sunlight. "Where are we?" Lila gasped, her heart racing.

"It feels... enchanted," Sam said, looking around in awe.

Just then, a loud thud echoed through the forest, shaking the ground beneath their feet. The friends turned to see a massive figure striding toward them—a giant, at least three times their size, with a bushy beard and clothes made from thick, woven fabric. "Well, well, what have we here?" the giant boomed, a curious glint in his eye.

"Uh, hello!" Sam stammered, feeling dwarfed by the giant's presence. "We're just... exploring?"

"Explorers, eh?" The giant chuckled, his voice rumbling like distant thunder. "You're in the land of the giants now! Name's Thorne. And you lot look a bit lost."

"Lost is an understatement," Jake said, his confidence waning. "We need to find a way back home."

"Ah, the portal! It's tricky to find," Thorne replied, scratching his beard thoughtfully. "You'll need to navigate through the Valley of Shadows, cross the River of Whispers, and finally reach the Mountain of Echoes to find your way back."

"Great," Mia sighed. "Just a casual stroll through dangerous territory, then."

"Fear not!" Thorne boomed, his eyes twinkling with mirth. "I'll guide you. It'll be an adventure, and I could use some company!"

Reluctantly but excitedly, the friends agreed, and with Thorne leading the way, they set off into the heart of the giant realm. As they traversed the lush landscapes, they encountered wonders beyond their wildest dreams—giant flowers that sang, waterfalls that sparkled like diamonds, and creatures that had yet to be discovered by human eyes.

But their journey was not without peril. In the Valley of Shadows, they faced menacing shadows that whispered their deepest fears. Each friend was tested: Jake confronted his fear of failure, Lila faced the pain of loss, and Sam battled his insecurities. With Thorne's guidance, they learned to confront their fears together, drawing strength from one another.

After navigating through the valley, they approached the River of Whispers, where the water shimmered with secrets. "To cross, you must reveal a truth about yourselves," Thorne instructed.

The friends gathered at the water's edge. Mia spoke first, her voice steady. "I've always been afraid of being alone, of losing my friends." As she confessed her fear, the river calmed, allowing them to cross safely.

One by one, they shared their truths, each confession strengthening their bond. When they finally reached the Mountain of Echoes, they were exhausted but filled with a newfound understanding of themselves and each other.

As they climbed the mountain, the echoes of their voices surrounded them, urging them to remember their journey. At the summit, they found a shimmering portal, but before stepping through, Thorne looked at them with a serious expression. "You've grown stronger, my friends. Remember, the power to overcome challenges lies not just in strength but in honesty and unity."

With heartfelt gratitude, they bid farewell to Thorne, stepping through the portal. The familiar woods of Millbrook welcomed them back, the archway shimmering one last time before fading from view.

As they emerged, the friends felt a sense of transformation. The mundane world around them seemed brighter, richer. They had faced giants—literal and metaphorical—and had emerged victorious.

"I guess we're not the same people we were before," Lila said, a smile on her face.

"No," Sam agreed, "we've learned that facing our fears together makes us stronger."

From that day forward, the friends cherished their bond, understanding that life's challenges were best faced with honesty, courage, and the support of those they loved. And as they wandered back into the familiar streets of Millbrook, they carried with them the echoes of their adventure, a reminder that even in the ordinary, the extraordinary awaits.

The Garden of Wishes

Nestled on the outskirts of the bustling town of Eldergrove lay a mysterious garden, shrouded in tales and whispered legends. Known as the Garden of Wishes, it was said that anyone who entered the garden could make a single wish, and it would be granted. However, the garden was also known for its tests, demanding sincerity and introspection from those who sought its magic. Over time, the garden became a forgotten myth, spoken of only in the hushed tones of elders around flickering fires.

One crisp autumn morning, Clara, a pragmatic woman in her thirties, found herself wandering through the golden leaves of the forest that bordered Eldergrove. She had come to the area seeking solace, escaping the pressures of her job and the weight of her unfulfilled dreams. A chance encounter with an elderly woman in town had rekindled her curiosity about the fabled garden, and she felt an inexplicable pull to discover it.

"Just beyond the willow trees, child," the old woman had said, her eyes twinkling with wisdom. "The garden will test your heart, but if you are true in your wish, you may find what you seek."

Determined, Clara followed the trail she had imagined the old woman describing, her heart racing with the thrill of possibility. After what felt like hours of wandering, she stumbled upon a clearing where the sunlight danced through the branches, illuminating a wooden archway entwined with ivy and flowers that shimmered in hues of blue and gold.

As she stepped through the archway, Clara felt a shift in the air, a gentle warmth enveloping her. Before her lay the Garden of Wishes, vibrant and lush, filled with flowers that seemed to hum with life and trees that whispered secrets in the wind. The scent of blooming jasmine and fresh earth intoxicated her senses, and for a moment, she was lost in the beauty of it all.

"Welcome, seeker," a voice echoed from the center of the garden. Clara turned to see a figure emerging from the shadows—a tall, elegant woman with flowing hair adorned with blossoms, her presence radiating grace and warmth.

"I am Isolde, the guardian of this garden," the woman said, her eyes glimmering like emeralds. "You may make one wish, but first, you must reflect on what it is you truly desire. The heart must be clear for the wish to be granted."

Clara hesitated, the weight of her thoughts swirling within her. She had always wished for success in her career, to be recognized for her hard work and creativity. Yet, beneath that desire lay a longing for something deeper—connection, happiness, and a sense of belonging.

"I want to be successful," she finally declared, but doubt lingered in her mind. "I want my art to be recognized."

Isolde smiled softly. "Art is a reflection of the soul. Are you certain that recognition is what you truly seek?"

Suddenly, the garden shimmered, and Clara found herself standing in a different setting—an elegant gallery filled with her artwork, people mingling and admiring her pieces. A sense of pride swelled within her. Yet, as she looked closer, she noticed the smiles felt hollow, and the conversations lacked depth. No one truly engaged with her, and she felt more isolated than ever.

"This is not what I want," she whispered, the weight of the realization heavy on her heart.

With a wave of her hand, Isolde returned Clara to the garden. "Reflect, dear one. What is it you truly desire?"

Clara took a deep breath, the beauty of the garden filling her senses. "I want to create art that connects with people, that brings them joy and comfort. I want to touch hearts, not just gain recognition."

"Then make your wish," Isolde encouraged, her voice like a soothing balm.

"I wish for the ability to create art that resonates deeply with others, art that heals and inspires," Clara declared, her voice steady and true.

As the words left her lips, a brilliant light enveloped her, filling the garden with a warm glow. She felt an overwhelming surge of energy coursing through her veins, and in that moment, Clara understood—the true magic of the garden lay not in the wish itself but in the clarity of her heart.

The light dimmed, and Clara found herself alone in the garden once more, the air still humming with energy. She could sense that something had changed within her, a newfound understanding of her purpose. Isolde appeared beside her, a satisfied smile on her face.

"You have chosen wisely, Clara. Your wish has been granted, but remember, the power to connect with others lies not just in your art but in your willingness to be vulnerable and genuine."

With a grateful heart, Clara left the garden, her mind alive with inspiration. Back in her studio, she poured herself into her work, creating pieces that conveyed raw emotion and authentic stories. The connections she formed with those who experienced her art deepened, and her pieces began to touch hearts in ways she had never imagined.

Months later, as she prepared for an exhibition, Clara reflected on her journey. The Garden of Wishes had not only granted her a powerful gift but had also taught her the importance of authenticity and connection. In the end, it wasn't the recognition she had sought, but the ability to inspire and heal through her art that brought her true fulfillment.

And as the opening night arrived, surrounded by friends, family, and strangers who had been touched by her creations, Clara understood that the greatest gift of all was the ability to connect with others and share in the human experience. The garden had revealed to her that true success was not merely about accolades but about the impact one could have on the lives of others.

The Star-Crossed Maiden

In the small village of Eldershire, where rolling hills kissed the sky and fields of wildflowers danced in the gentle breeze, tales of falling stars were a common bedtime story. Villagers would gather on clear nights, their eyes turned skyward, wishing on the shooting stars that streaked across the firmament. Little did they know that one such star, destined to fall, held the power to change their lives forever.

One fateful evening, as the sun dipped below the horizon, a brilliant star tore through the night sky, trailing silver light like a comet. It arced gracefully before crashing into the dense woods surrounding Eldershire, leaving a plume of sparkling dust in its wake. The villagers watched in awe, their hearts filled with wonder and anticipation.

Among them was a young woman named Elara, known for her wild spirit and dreams that reached beyond the confines of her village. She felt a peculiar pull toward the woods, a whispering promise that something extraordinary awaited her. Driven by curiosity, Elara ventured into the trees, her heart racing with excitement.

As she approached the impact site, the air shimmered with ethereal energy. There, amid the shimmering dust, lay a beautiful maiden, her long hair cascading like molten silver and her skin glowing with an otherworldly radiance. Elara knelt beside her, captivated by the maiden's beauty and the strange familiarity in her eyes.

"Are you alright?" Elara asked, her voice barely a whisper.

The maiden opened her eyes, revealing iridescent depths that sparkled like the night sky. "I am Lyra," she replied, her voice melodic and soothing. "I have fallen from the heavens, a star now taking form as a mortal."

Elara's heart skipped a beat, awestruck by the maiden's presence. "A fallen star? How is that possible?"

Lyra smiled, a hint of sadness dancing in her expression. "I was once part of the cosmos, a guide for lost souls. But I longed to experience life as a human, to understand the emotions that bind us all. In my yearning, I fell, but my journey comes with a price."

"What kind of price?" Elara inquired, intrigued yet cautious.

"I carry a hidden past," Lyra confessed, her gaze turning distant. "In my desire to know love and connection, I broke a celestial law. Now, I must choose between remaining in this form or returning to the stars, for the magic that binds me to this world will only last for a brief time."

Elara felt a surge of empathy for the fallen star. "You shouldn't have to choose! You deserve to live freely, to explore this world."

"But freedom comes with sacrifice," Lyra replied, her expression turning somber. "If I choose to stay, I will lose my connection to the stars and the magic that flows through me. I will become just like everyone else, bound by the limitations of mortality."

Determined to help her newfound friend, Elara proposed a plan. "Let's seek the village elders. They may know of a way to help you retain your magic while living as a human."

Lyra hesitated but eventually nodded. "Very well. If there is hope, I will follow you."

The two women made their way back to the village, Lyra's ethereal beauty drawing the eyes of the villagers. They arrived at the elder's home, a weathered cottage adorned with herbs and charms. The elders gathered around as Elara explained Lyra's predicament.

Elder Morwen, a wise woman with silver hair, listened intently. "Magic is a delicate balance, dear child," she said thoughtfully. "To retain one's powers while living as a human is rare and requires a profound act of selflessness."

"What must we do?" Elara asked, determination blazing in her heart.

"To bind Lyra's essence to the heart of the forest," Elder Morwen explained, "she must perform an act of pure love—sacrificing something dear to her. Only then can she maintain her magic while embracing her humanity."

Lyra's heart sank. "But what could I possibly sacrifice?"

As the sun dipped below the horizon, casting a warm glow over the village, Elara pondered the solution. "Your connection to the stars," she suggested gently. "If you truly desire to live among us, perhaps letting go of your celestial ties is the sacrifice you must make."

Lyra's expression shifted, pain etched across her face. "To give up my past... it would mean losing a part of myself."

"But you would gain a new life, filled with experiences and relationships," Elara urged. "You would be free to create your own destiny."

With tears shimmering in her eyes, Lyra nodded slowly. "I will do it. I will sacrifice my celestial essence for the chance to embrace the beauty of this world."

The villagers gathered, forming a circle around the two women as Lyra raised her arms to the heavens. A soft glow enveloped her, and as she chanted words of farewell, the sky above shimmered, stars flickering like distant memories. The air hummed with energy, and the villagers watched in awe as Lyra's essence began to shift, her celestial light intertwining with the earth around them.

In that moment of sacrifice, Lyra felt a profound sense of peace wash over her. As the last remnants of her starry essence faded, a brilliant light erupted from her heart, intertwining with the trees and flowers, binding her spirit to the very essence of the forest.

The villagers erupted in applause, celebrating Lyra's transformation. She smiled, the warmth of their acceptance filling her with joy. Though she had sacrificed her celestial magic, she had gained something far more precious—a place in this world, woven into the fabric of life itself.

As days turned into weeks, Lyra embraced her new existence in Eldershire, discovering the simple joys of human life. She formed deep connections with the villagers, shared laughter, and experienced love in its many forms. The sacrifices she had made had opened her heart to the world around her.

And so, the lesson of Lyra's journey spread throughout the village: that true magic lies not in power or celestial origins, but in the bonds we forge and the love we share. For in giving up a part of herself, Lyra discovered that she had gained everything—life, connection, and the beauty of being truly alive.

Wings of Fire

In the mystical land of Drakoria, where emerald forests kissed the horizon and mountains loomed high above the clouds, dragon-riding was both an art and a rite of passage. The bond between rider and dragon was sacred, forged through trust and understanding, and those who mastered this skill were celebrated as heroes. Among the hopefuls was a young man named Finn, with dreams as vast as the skies he yearned to conquer.

Finn had grown up listening to tales of legendary dragon riders and their breathtaking flights over the kingdom. He had always felt an undeniable connection to the dragons, their fiery spirits resonating with his own. But his journey was not without challenges. Orphaned at a young age, Finn had spent his childhood in the shadow of doubt, yearning to prove himself worthy of a dragon's trust.

One bright morning, with determination burning in his chest, Finn traveled to the renowned Dragonspire Academy, where aspiring riders trained under the watchful eyes of seasoned veterans. The academy was nestled atop a cliff, overlooking the vast expanse of the kingdom. As he climbed the stone steps, he could hear the roars of dragons and the laughter of riders echoing through the air.

Upon entering the academy, Finn felt a mixture of excitement and trepidation. He joined a group of other students, each one eager to impress the instructors and earn the bond of a dragon. The first lesson began with the basics of dragon communication, teaching them to understand the unique body language and vocalizations of the majestic creatures.

As the weeks passed, Finn trained tirelessly, learning to harness his innate abilities and develop a deep connection with dragons. He faced challenges that tested his resolve—endless drills, simulated battles, and daring escapes from mock dragon attacks. Yet, despite his efforts, he struggled to find a dragon willing to bond with him.

"Patience, Finn," his instructor, a seasoned rider named Elysia, advised. "A dragon chooses its rider based on trust and compatibility. You must open your heart."

Frustrated but determined, Finn ventured into the wilds surrounding the academy, seeking a dragon that would accept him. One fateful afternoon, he stumbled upon a hidden valley bathed in sunlight, where a lone dragon lay resting—a magnificent creature with iridescent scales that shimmered like gems.

"Hello, great one," Finn called softly, approaching the dragon with reverence. "I wish to ride with you."

The dragon, sensing his sincerity, opened its eyes, revealing pools of molten gold. "Why should I bond with you, young human?" it asked, its voice rumbling like distant thunder.

Finn took a deep breath, heart pounding. "Because I seek not power, but a connection—a partnership where we both thrive."

The dragon regarded him thoughtfully, its gaze piercing through Finn's façade. "Many seek power; few seek understanding. Prove your worth, and I may consider your request."

Determined to earn the dragon's respect, Finn spent the next several days in the valley, learning the ways of the dragon. He gathered herbs for healing, helped with maintenance of the dragon's lair, and listened to the ancient stories whispered in the winds. Slowly, a bond began to form between them, built on trust and mutual respect.

One day, while exploring the valley, a dark storm rolled in unexpectedly. Finn sensed danger and rushed to the dragon's side. "We must prepare for the worst! We can face this together!"

The dragon looked at him, recognizing the strength in his resolve. "Very well, let us see if you are truly worthy."

As the storm unleashed its fury, Finn climbed onto the dragon's back, gripping tightly as the creature took to the skies. They soared above the turbulent clouds, battling the howling winds and lashing rain. In that moment, Finn felt alive, adrenaline coursing through him as they danced with the storm.

But as they flew, Finn noticed a dark figure emerging from the clouds—an enemy dragon rider, wielding dark magic and intent on destruction. The rider unleashed a torrent of fire, targeting Finn and his companion. In that moment of chaos, Finn remembered Elysia's teachings about harnessing the bond between rider and dragon.

"Trust me!" Finn shouted to the dragon, focusing his energy on their connection. "We can overcome this together!"

Drawing upon their newfound partnership, they dodged the flames, executing maneuvers that seemed impossible. Finn guided the dragon, their movements fluid and harmonious. In a final burst of energy, they unleashed a powerful blast of fire together, driving back the enemy rider and forcing him to retreat into the storm.

As they descended back into the valley, the storm began to clear. Finn felt exhilarated, yet he realized that this victory was not just about power; it was about the bond they had forged through trust and understanding.

The dragon landed gracefully, and Finn dismounted, breathless with awe. "You chose me!" he exclaimed, joy radiating from him.

The dragon nodded, its golden eyes gleaming with approval. "You have proven yourself worthy, Finn. Together, we will soar to heights beyond imagination."

As word of their triumph spread throughout the academy, Finn was hailed as a hero. He had not only bonded with a dragon but had also learned the invaluable lesson of humility and trust.

In time, Finn and his dragon became legends in their own right, defenders of Drakoria. But Finn never forgot the importance of their bond, understanding that true strength lies not just in power, but in the connections forged through trust, understanding, and the willingness to face challenges together.

And as they soared through the skies, the winds whispering their names, Finn knew he had found his place among the stars, where dreams take flight on the wings of fire.

The Awakening of Thalassa

In the heart of the stormy sea, where waves crashed violently against jagged cliffs, legends spoke of a forgotten kingdom that lay beneath the ocean's depths. Known as Thalassa, it was said to be a realm of unparalleled beauty, ruled by merfolk who wielded the magic of the tides. For centuries, the kingdom had been lost to time, submerged under the waves after a great cataclysm. But the whispers of its existence lingered, igniting the imaginations of sailors and dreamers alike.

One such dreamer was a woman named Elenora. A marine archaeologist by trade, she had spent years studying the myths surrounding Thalassa, convinced that the lost kingdom was more than just a story. With a heart full of hope and a determination fueled by her childhood dreams, she assembled a crew and set sail aboard her small ship, *The Sea Whisperer*.

"Remember, the sea holds secrets we may not be prepared for," her first mate, Jonah, cautioned as they departed from the harbor. His weathered face bore the marks of experience, but Elenora felt the thrill of adventure overshadowing any fear.

Days turned into weeks as they navigated treacherous waters, battling storms and braving the unpredictable whims of the ocean. Finally, one moonlit night, as the stars twinkled like diamonds above, they stumbled upon a shimmering patch of water that glowed with an otherworldly light.

"Look!" Elenora exclaimed, her eyes wide with wonder. "It's beautiful!"

As they approached the glowing waters, a soft melody floated through the air, weaving around them like a gentle caress. It beckoned them closer, and Elenora felt an undeniable pull toward the enchanting sound.

Suddenly, the ocean surged, and before their eyes, the waters parted, revealing the silhouette of a grand city rising from the depths. Towers of coral and crystal glimmered under the moonlight, and intricate sculptures adorned the architecture, each more breathtaking than the last.

"This... this is Thalassa," Elenora breathed, overwhelmed by the sight.

As they anchored the ship and descended into the underwater kingdom, the air around them shimmered with magic. Merfolk emerged from the shadows, their scales reflecting the light like precious jewels. One among them, a regal figure with flowing hair the color of seafoam, stepped forward.

"I am Queen Marella of Thalassa," she announced, her voice echoing like the gentle lapping of waves. "You have awakened our kingdom from its slumber. For centuries, we have waited for the right souls to return and restore the balance of the ocean."

Elenora's heart raced. "We came seeking the truth of your kingdom. What happened to Thalassa?"

"A great betrayal led to our downfall," Marella explained, her eyes filled with sorrow. "An ancient artifact, the Heart of the Ocean, was stolen by a power-hungry sorcerer. In his greed, he unleashed a cataclysm that submerged our home. Only those pure of heart can return it to us."

With a shared look of determination, Elenora and her crew pledged to help the merfolk recover the Heart of the Ocean. Guided by Marella, they ventured through the vibrant streets of Thalassa, witnessing the beauty and despair that lingered in its depths.

As they traveled, Elenora learned of the sorcerer who had betrayed the kingdom, a former guardian turned tyrant, now hiding in the shadowy depths of the Abyssal Trench. "We must confront him," Marella urged. "He holds the key to our revival."

Elenora and her crew, now intertwined with the fate of Thalassa, prepared for the journey into the dark unknown. As they approached the trench, the water grew colder, and an unsettling silence enveloped them. Shadows flickered in the periphery, and the feeling of dread hung heavily in the water.

Upon reaching the depths of the trench, they encountered the sorcerer, a figure cloaked in darkness, his eyes glowing with malice. "You dare challenge me?" he sneered, his voice dripping with contempt. "You cannot fathom the power I wield!"

"We seek the Heart of the Ocean," Elenora declared, her voice strong despite her fear. "You will return it to the merfolk."

The sorcerer laughed, a sound that echoed like thunder. "Power is not given; it is taken! You are fools to think you can stop me!"

As he unleashed a torrent of dark magic, the waters roiled around them. But in that moment, Elenora felt a surge of energy from the merfolk beside her. "Together!" Marella cried, her voice rising above the chaos.

Drawing upon their combined strength, Elenora and the merfolk countered the sorcerer's magic. The waters shimmered, the Heart of the Ocean pulsing with light, and in a blinding flash, they overwhelmed the darkness.

As the shadows dissipated, the sorcerer's power crumbled, revealing the Heart of the Ocean, a radiant gem glowing with life. "No!" he bellowed, but it was too late. The gem was reclaimed by Marella, who held it high above her head, its brilliance illuminating the trench.

In that moment, the kingdom of Thalassa began to transform. The waters shimmered with life, the coral glowed brighter, and the sorrow that had once settled over the city lifted like a heavy fog. The kingdom was reborn.

With the sorcerer defeated and the Heart restored, Elenora stood beside Marella, witnessing the miracle of rebirth. "Thank you," Marella said, her voice filled with gratitude. "You have not only saved our kingdom but restored the balance of the ocean."

As Elenora prepared to leave, she felt a strange longing. "Will we ever return?" she asked, a hint of sadness in her voice.

"Your hearts are forever tied to this kingdom," Marella replied, her eyes sparkling. "Remember, true power lies in connection and understanding, not dominance."

As the waters began to swirl around them, Elenora felt the magic of Thalassa envelop her, and in an instant, she and her crew were back on their ship, the sun rising over the horizon. They gazed at one another, awed by the adventure they had shared.

In the days that followed, Elenora carried the lessons of Thalassa with her. She understood that the true heart of power resided not in possession but in the bonds formed through shared experiences. And though they had left the underwater kingdom, its magic lived on in her heart, a reminder that even in darkness, hope could rise like the tide, bringing life and light to all.

Beneath the Surface

In the bustling city of Verenthia, where skyscrapers pierced the clouds and neon lights flickered like stars, a shape-shifter named Kael lived a double life. By day, he was an unassuming barista in a small coffee shop, blending in with the hum of humanity. But when the moon rose high and the shadows deepened, Kael would transform into a sleek black panther, prowling the alleys and rooftops of the city, embracing the freedom that came with his true nature.

Kael had learned long ago to keep his abilities a secret. Humans, with their fears and prejudices, would never understand. So he wore a mask of normalcy, diligently serving cappuccinos and pastries while carefully observing the lives of the people around him. Yet, every time he glanced out of the shop window, he felt a pull—a yearning for a connection he could never fully grasp.

One fateful evening, while closing the shop, Kael noticed a woman standing outside, her dark hair blowing gently in the night breeze. She had an air of mystery about her, and as their eyes met, something sparked between them. Intrigued, Kael stepped outside, curiosity bubbling within him.

"Hi, I'm Kael," he said, a friendly smile on his face.

"Amara," she replied, her voice soft yet captivating. "I've seen you here before. You have a knack for making the best lattes."

"Thanks! It's a passion of mine," Kael said, trying to hide his nerves. He felt an unusual connection with Amara, a warmth that made him forget the secret he was harboring.

As they talked, Kael found himself drawn to her. Amara shared stories of her travels, her dreams, and the world beyond Verenthia. Kael felt a flutter in his chest, a longing to reveal his true self but held back by the fear of rejection.

Over the next few weeks, their friendship blossomed. They shared laughter, long conversations, and quiet moments in the coffee shop, and Kael began to entertain the idea of letting Amara into his secret world. But doubts lingered—what if she didn't accept him for who he truly was?

One night, after an exhilarating evening spent under the stars, Kael invited Amara to join him on a late-night adventure. "There's something I want to show you," he said, excitement dancing in his eyes.

"Lead the way," Amara replied, her curiosity piqued.

They ventured to a secluded park on the outskirts of the city, where the sound of the bustling streets faded into the background. The moon bathed the area in silver light, illuminating the path ahead. Kael felt the familiar urge to shift, to embrace the wild spirit within him.

"Wait here for a moment," he said, his heart pounding. He stepped behind a large tree, allowing the magic to envelop him. In seconds, he transformed into a sleek black panther, feeling the rush of power coursing through his veins.

Emerging from the shadows, he approached Amara, who gasped in awe. "Kael! Is that you?" she exclaimed, her voice a mixture of surprise and delight.

He nuzzled her hand, relishing her touch, and in that moment, he felt a surge of freedom. This was who he truly was. But just as he reveled in the connection, a shiver of fear washed over him. "What if she's afraid?" he thought.

Amara knelt beside him, her eyes shining with wonder. "You're beautiful," she said softly. "I can't believe it. You're a shape-shifter!"

Kael transformed back into his human form, vulnerability creeping in as he met her gaze. "I wanted to show you who I really am, but I was afraid. I didn't know how you'd react."

Instead of fear, Amara's expression softened. "I think it's incredible. You're amazing, Kael. I've always felt there was more to you than met the eye."

As they embraced, Kael felt a weight lift from his shoulders. "I've spent so long hiding," he admitted. "I feared rejection more than anything."

Amara stepped back, her eyes searching his. "You shouldn't have to hide. We all have secrets, but it's the connections we build that truly matter."

Just then, the peaceful atmosphere shifted as a shadow flickered at the edge of the park. From the darkness emerged a group of hooded figures, their eyes gleaming with malicious intent. "We've found you at last, shape-shifter," the leader sneered. "Time to pay for your deceit."

Kael's heart raced. "Run, Amara!" he shouted, pushing her away from the encroaching danger.

"No! I won't leave you!" she cried, her voice fierce with defiance.

The hooded figures moved closer, their intentions clear. Kael felt the instinct to shift returning, but this time it was different. "Stay close to me," he said, standing protectively in front of her. As the figures lunged, Kael transformed once more into the panther, and in that moment, he understood the power of his bond with Amara.

Together, they fought against the assailants. Amara, armed with a small dagger she had concealed in her boot, fought alongside Kael, her movements fluid and courageous. The two of them became a whirlwind of strength and unity, pushing back the dark figures until they fled into the night.

Once the threat had passed, Kael shifted back, breathing heavily. "I never wanted to drag you into my world," he admitted, his voice trembling.

Amara placed her hand on his shoulder. "You didn't drag me anywhere, Kael. I chose to stand with you. This is who you are, and I respect that. I wish for you to be who you are, and I want to be part of your life."

In that moment, Kael understood the lesson he had learned through their ordeal. True strength did not lie in concealing one's identity or living in fear; it was about embracing who he was and allowing others to see him, flaws and all. The connection he had forged with Amara was a reminder that love and trust could blossom even in the darkest of times.

As dawn broke over the horizon, painting the sky with hues of gold and pink, Kael knew that he had found something far more valuable than he had ever imagined. He had not only shared his secret but had gained a partner to face the world with. Together, they would navigate the challenges ahead, side by side, united by the strength of their bond.

The Dragon's Choice

In the heart of the Kingdom of Eldoria, a foreboding tower rose against the sky, its stones worn by the passage of time. This was no ordinary tower; it was the prison of Princess Selene, locked away by a wicked sorcerer whose magic had corrupted the land. Guarding the tower was a fearsome dragon named Ignis, known for his fiery breath and fierce loyalty to his master. Many knights had attempted to rescue the princess, but none had returned, leaving the kingdom in despair.

Among those who dared to take up the challenge was Sir Cedric, a knight renowned for his bravery but burdened by the weight of his own insecurities. "I must do this," he whispered to himself as he prepared for the quest. "Not just for the princess, but for my own honor." With a gleaming sword at his side and determination in his heart, he set off toward the ominous tower.

The journey was fraught with peril, filled with treacherous paths and whispering shadows. Yet, as he approached the tower, Cedric's heart raced not with fear but with a sense of purpose. He had spent years living in the shadow of greater knights, always feeling inadequate. But this quest could change everything.

As Cedric reached the foot of the tower, he felt the ground tremble beneath him. Ignis, the dragon, appeared, his scales glinting in the sunlight like molten gold. "Halt, knight!" the dragon roared, smoke curling from his nostrils. "Turn back now, or face the flames of my wrath!"

Cedric stood tall, gripping his sword. "I have come to rescue Princess Selene. I will not back down."

The dragon's laughter rumbled through the air. "Many have come before you, brave knight. What makes you think you are any different?"

"Because I believe in my cause," Cedric replied, his voice steady despite the uncertainty swirling within him. "I fight not just for glory but for the freedom of the princess and the hope of this kingdom."

Ignis regarded him with a curious glint in his eyes. "A noble sentiment, but words mean little against fire. If you wish to pass, you must face my challenge."

"Name it," Cedric declared, resolve hardening within him.

"I will ask you three questions," Ignis said, his tone shifting to one of seriousness. "Answer truthfully, and you may proceed. Fail, and you shall become another lost knight."

The first question came swiftly. "What is the greatest strength of a knight?"

Cedric thought for a moment, recalling the stories of honor and valor he had been told as a boy. "The greatest strength of a knight lies in his heart. It is compassion and courage that guide him, not just the blade he wields."

"Correct," Ignis acknowledged, his eyes narrowing. "The second question: What is the greatest weakness of a knight?"

Cedric hesitated, realizing the weight of this question. "Doubt," he finally said. "When a knight loses faith in himself, he becomes blind to his purpose and unable to protect those who rely on him."

Ignis nodded, and Cedric felt a swell of confidence. "Two correct answers. Now for the final question: What do you seek most in this world?"

This question struck at the core of Cedric's journey. He had spent so long seeking approval and glory, but now he understood the truth of his heart. "I seek purpose, not just for myself but to bring hope to others. I want to be a knight who inspires courage in those who feel lost."

Silence enveloped the clearing as Ignis pondered Cedric's words. "You have answered wisely, knight. Your heart is true. You may pass."

As Cedric ascended the tower's spiraling stairs, he felt the air grow heavy with magic. At the top, he found Princess Selene, her beauty radiant despite the shadows that lingered around her. "You came," she whispered, hope illuminating her eyes.

"Of course," Cedric replied, rushing to her side. "I will get you out of here."

As he attempted to unlock her chains, Selene grasped his arm. "Wait! The sorcerer's magic binds me here. You cannot simply free me; the spell must be broken."

Cedric felt a knot of dread in his stomach. "Then how can I save you?"

"Only by confronting the sorcerer himself can we break the curse," Selene replied, determination flooding her voice.

With renewed resolve, Cedric took Selene's hand, and together they descended the tower, ready to face the sorcerer. As they reached the ground, Ignis awaited them, his eyes narrowing with interest.

"You have chosen wisely, knight," Ignis said, his voice low. "But know that confronting the sorcerer will not be easy. He will test you in ways you cannot foresee."

Together, Cedric, Selene, and Ignis journeyed to the sorcerer's lair, an ominous fortress surrounded by dark clouds and crackling energy. As they approached, a wave of dread washed over them, but Cedric steeled his resolve.

Inside the fortress, the sorcerer awaited, cloaked in shadows. "A knight and a princess," he sneered. "What an amusing pair. Do you truly believe you can defeat me?"

Cedric stepped forward, gripping his sword tightly. "We seek to free the kingdom from your tyranny."

The sorcerer's laughter echoed through the chamber. "You are naive. Power comes at a cost. You cannot comprehend the depths of my magic."

With a flick of his wrist, the sorcerer unleashed dark tendrils of magic that lashed out at them. But Cedric, filled with determination and the support of Selene and Ignis, stood his ground. "We will not back down! Your reign ends here!"

In a fierce battle that shook the very foundations of the fortress, Cedric fought with all his heart. With each swing of his sword, he remembered the lessons Ignis had taught him. As the tide turned in their favor, Selene used her own magic, channeling the light that had been hidden within her. Together, they faced the sorcerer, their combined strength illuminating the darkness.

Finally, with one last surge of energy, Cedric struck true, breaking the sorcerer's hold over the fortress. As the shadows dissipated, the sorcerer vanished with a shriek, leaving only silence in his wake.

Breathing heavily, Cedric and Selene emerged victorious, and as the sun broke through the dark clouds, the kingdom of Eldoria began to heal. The power of hope had triumphed over fear.

As they stood together, Cedric turned to Selene. "You were right. I found my purpose not in seeking glory, but in the bonds we forged in this battle."

Selene smiled, her eyes bright. "Together, we can inspire change and bring hope to those who need it most."

And with that, the young knight, the brave princess, and the wise dragon embarked on a new journey—not just as heroes of the realm but as symbols of unity and the power of believing in one another.

The Storm of Transcendence

The village of Elden Hollow lay nestled in a verdant valley, a patchwork of thatched roofs and cobblestone streets, where the seasons danced in harmony. Life was simple and serene, yet beneath the surface, a sense of longing simmered among its residents. They often whispered about the tales of travelers who spoke of worlds beyond their own—worlds filled with magic, wonder, and boundless possibilities.

One stormy evening, the sky darkened unnaturally, swirling with ominous clouds that seemed to pulse with energy. A fierce wind whipped through the village, rattling shutters and sending leaves spiraling into the air. Elden Hollow had seen storms before, but this one felt different, charged with an inexplicable magic that sent shivers down the spines of its inhabitants.

In the heart of the village, a curious woman named Lira stood outside her cottage, gazing at the roiling clouds. With her wild auburn hair dancing in the wind and her emerald eyes sparkling with curiosity, she felt a deep pull toward the storm. "Something is happening," she murmured, her heart racing with anticipation.

As the wind howled, the ground trembled, and a blinding flash of lightning illuminated the sky. Suddenly, a colossal whirlwind descended from the heavens, engulfing the village in a spiral of shimmering light. The villagers screamed and clutched one another, fear rippling through the crowd as they were lifted off their feet.

"Hold on!" Lira shouted, her voice barely audible over the chaos. In an instant, the village vanished from its familiar surroundings, replaced by a kaleidoscope of colors and shapes that swirled around them. The world blurred, and time seemed to stand still.

When the storm finally subsided, Elden Hollow found itself on the edge of a vast and alien landscape. They stood amidst towering trees with bioluminescent leaves, their glow casting an enchanting light over the terrain. Strange creatures flitted between the branches, and the air was thick with the scent of vibrant flowers that pulsed like a heartbeat.

"What just happened?" whispered Tomas, the village blacksmith, his hands trembling as he clutched his hammer.

"We've been transported to another dimension!" Lira exclaimed, her eyes wide with wonder. "This is incredible!"

The villagers were torn between fear and excitement, but curiosity won out. Together, they ventured deeper into this magical realm, guided by Lira's unwavering spirit. They soon discovered that this dimension was filled with extraordinary sights: rivers of liquid crystal, mountains that sparkled like diamonds, and skies that shifted in hue with every passing moment.

As they explored, they stumbled upon a group of creatures resembling tall, ethereal beings with luminescent skin and flowing garments that shimmered like starlight. They approached the villagers, their voices melodic and soothing.

"Welcome, travelers from the realm of mortals," one of the beings spoke, its eyes twinkling like distant stars. "We are the Luminara, guardians of this dimension. You have been brought here for a purpose."

"What purpose?" Lira asked, her heart pounding with anticipation.

"The storm you encountered was a rare phenomenon," the Luminara explained. "It opens a gateway for those seeking change and transformation. You have the power to reshape your destinies, but first, you must confront the shadows of your past."

As they spoke, visions began to swirl around the villagers, revealing moments from their lives—their regrets, their fears, the paths not taken. Each villager was faced with a reflection of their choices, laid bare before them.

Tomas stepped forward, trembling. "What do you mean by shadows?"

"Each of you must face the darkness that holds you back," the Luminara replied gently. "Only by embracing your truths can you harness the magic of this realm."

Lira felt a surge of resolve. "I've always wanted to be more than just a villager," she confessed, her voice steady. "I wanted to explore the world, to create art that inspires others."

One by one, the villagers voiced their fears and aspirations, confronting the parts of themselves they had buried deep. With each admission, the air around them pulsed with energy, the ground shimmering as the Luminara absorbed their truths.

As the final villager, Tomas, shared his insecurities about never living up to his father's legacy, a brilliant light enveloped them all. The Luminara nodded, their faces reflecting pride and understanding.

"You have faced your shadows," one of them said. "Now, you have the power to shape this dimension to your will. What will you create?"

Eager anticipation filled the air as Lira turned to the villagers. "Let's create a world where we can be our true selves, where we can pursue our dreams without fear!"

With newfound purpose, the villagers focused their collective energy, envisioning a vibrant world. As they did, the landscape around them transformed, blossoming with life, color, and possibilities. Fields of flowers bloomed in radiant hues, rivers sparkled with laughter, and the sky shimmered with hope.

As the magic settled, the Luminara smiled. "You have embraced your power. Now, you must decide: do you wish to stay in this realm, or return to Elden Hollow with your newfound wisdom?"

The villagers exchanged glances, their hearts heavy with the choice. Lira took a deep breath, understanding the weight of the decision. "We have learned that our fears do not define us, and we carry this strength back home."

With a wave of their hands, the Luminara opened a portal back to Elden Hollow. The villagers stepped through, filled with hope and determination. As the familiar sights of their village came into view, they felt different—changed.

From that day forward, Elden Hollow thrived with newfound energy. The villagers pursued their passions, supported one another in their journeys, and transformed their community into a tapestry of dreams realized.

And as Lira stood beneath the twilight sky, she gazed at the stars, remembering the Luminara and the power they had discovered within themselves. She knew that true magic lay not in distant realms but in the courage to face their shadows and embrace their true selves.

The Chosen Flame

In the heart of the Kingdom of Eldoria, a sense of foreboding hung in the air. The ancient prophecy of the Chosen One, a figure destined to bring balance to the realm, had been whispered for generations. It spoke of a child born under a blood moon, one who would wield the power to unite the fractured lands and vanquish the darkness that threatened to consume them all. Yet, as the years passed and the skies darkened, the kingdom's hope waned, and the prophecy became a mere legend.

In the quaint village of Briarwood, a young woman named Mira lived a quiet life, tending to her family's small farm. With auburn hair that danced in the wind and eyes that sparkled with curiosity, she felt a restless energy within her—a yearning for something greater. Every evening, as she gazed up at the stars, she wondered if the tales of the Chosen One were true and if she was somehow destined for more.

One fateful night, as a blood moon rose high above the horizon, an unearthly glow enveloped the village. Mira awoke to a soft whisper in her dreams, a voice that beckoned her to the woods beyond her home. Drawn by an unseen force, she slipped from her bed and ventured into the night.

The woods were alive with magic, the air thick with the scent of wildflowers and the hum of ancient energy. As she followed the path illuminated by moonlight, Mira stumbled upon an ancient stone altar, covered in ivy and glowing with a soft luminescence. At its center lay a small, ornate box adorned with intricate carvings.

Curiosity piqued, Mira approached the altar and gently opened the box. Inside was a shimmering crystal that pulsed with warmth and light, filling her heart with a sense of belonging. As she touched the crystal, a vision enveloped her—she saw a vast battlefield, a dark figure looming over a fallen king, and then, a glimpse of herself standing tall, radiant with power.

"Mira," the voice of the forest whispered, "you are the Chosen One. The prophecy has awakened within you."

Stunned, Mira stumbled back, grappling with the enormity of the revelation. "Me? But I'm just a farmer's daughter!" she protested, fear and disbelief flooding her heart.

"Your lineage is intertwined with the magic of this realm," the voice continued. "Only you can harness the Flame of Unity, the very essence that binds the kingdoms together. Embrace your destiny, or darkness will prevail."

Mira stood frozen, the weight of the world settling on her shoulders. As the moonlight faded, she realized she had a choice to make. In the days that followed, she trained diligently, honing her abilities under the guidance of the ancient spirits of the forest. Each lesson revealed more about the power within her, and with it, the knowledge of her purpose.

However, the darkness was not idle. The sorcerer Malakar, a figure shrouded in shadows, had been searching for the Chosen One to extinguish the flame of hope. His influence spread like a plague across the kingdoms, igniting discord and fear among the people.

As Mira prepared to confront Malakar, she gathered a small band of allies—brave souls who believed in her cause. Together, they journeyed to the heart of Eldoria, where the final battle loomed. Along the way, they encountered fierce creatures and treacherous terrain, but each challenge only strengthened their bond and resolve.

The day of reckoning arrived, and the sky darkened as they approached Malakar's fortress. The air crackled with tension, and Mira felt the weight of the prophecy pressing upon her. She led her friends into the heart of the darkness, where Malakar awaited, a sinister grin stretched across his face.

"So, the little flame has come to play," he sneered, his voice echoing through the chamber. "You think you can defeat me?"

"I will not let you extinguish hope," Mira declared, her heart pounding as she stepped forward. As she held the crystal aloft, it blazed with light, illuminating the chamber and pushing back the shadows that clung to the walls.

Malakar unleashed a torrent of dark magic, but Mira stood firm, channeling the energy of the Flame of Unity. As the two forces collided, the very fabric of reality trembled. In that moment, she realized that the prophecy wasn't merely about her power; it was about the strength that lay in unity, in the bonds forged through shared struggles.

With a fierce cry, she summoned the combined will of her allies and the essence of the crystal. The light expanded, engulfing Malakar in a blaze of brilliance. "You will not win," she shouted, her voice unwavering. "The darkness cannot thrive where there is hope!"

As the light consumed Malakar, he screamed in fury, the shadows dissipating like mist before the dawn. When the brilliance faded, the chamber lay silent, and Mira stood victorious, the remnants of the darkness fading from the land.

As the sun broke through the clouds, illuminating Eldoria in golden light, Mira felt the weight of her journey settle into her heart. She had not only fulfilled the prophecy but had also discovered the truth behind it—the Chosen One was not simply a figure of power, but a vessel of unity, a beacon of hope that thrived when hearts joined together.

From that day forward, Mira continued to nurture the bonds of the kingdom, guiding its people toward harmony. And as the stories of her bravery spread, she learned that true strength lay not in individual might but in the willingness to embrace the light within each other. Together, they rebuilt their world, creating a legacy that would echo through generations—a reminder that even in the darkest times, unity could kindle the brightest flame.

The Elixir of Ambrosia

In the quaint village of Eldergrove, nestled between lush green hills and shimmering streams, life moved at a leisurely pace. The villagers often whispered about old tales—of witches, magical potions, and the enchantments that could change one's fate. Among them lived a modest herbalist named Elinora, known for her potions and remedies. Her small apothecary was filled with jars of herbs, colorful powders, and mysterious concoctions, each with its own purpose.

One afternoon, as Elinora was sorting through her supplies, she stumbled upon a tattered scroll hidden beneath a stack of dusty books. Curiosity piqued, she unrolled it and discovered a recipe for a potion called the Elixir of Ambrosia—a potion said to grant extraordinary powers for a single day. The scroll promised that one sip would bestow the drinker with unmatched strength, wisdom, or agility, depending on their heart's desire.

Elinora felt a twinge of excitement. "What if it's true?" she thought. "What could I achieve with such power?" The temptation of the elixir tugged at her, but she also felt the weight of responsibility. Power, after all, could be a double-edged sword.

As dusk fell, she decided to prepare the potion, drawn by the thrill of possibility. Gathering the ingredients—a rare flower that bloomed only under the full moon, crushed dragonfruit for vitality, and a drop of dew collected from the highest peak—she meticulously followed the recipe. The mixture bubbled and glowed a vibrant gold, filling the room with a tantalizing aroma.

After hours of preparation, Elinora finally held the small vial in her hand, the liquid shimmering like sunlight. "What will it be?" she mused, contemplating her desires. In her heart, she knew she wanted to make a difference in the village, to protect it from the shadows that threatened to encroach upon their peaceful lives.

With a deep breath, she raised the vial to her lips and drank the elixir in one swift motion. A warm sensation enveloped her, and for a moment, she felt weightless, as if she were floating above the ground. The world around her sharpened into focus, colors brightening and sounds amplifying, filling her with a rush of energy.

"Extraordinary," she whispered, feeling the power coursing through her veins. Elinora decided to test her newfound abilities. With a single leap, she vaulted through the door and into the moonlit night, landing gracefully on the cobblestone path.

As she ran through the village, she felt invincible. She could hear the whispers of the wind, see the smallest details of the night, and her heart raced with exhilaration. In that moment, Elinora resolved to use her powers for good.

As she approached the village square, she noticed a commotion. A group of bandits had taken advantage of the night, ransacking the market stalls and threatening the villagers. Without hesitation, Elinora sprang into action, feeling the strength of the elixir surge within her.

With agility that left her breathless, she darted between the bandits, distracting them with swift movements and calculated strikes. The bandits were taken aback by her unexpected prowess. With every movement, she felt the elixir guiding her, her body responding effortlessly.

"Leave this place!" she shouted, her voice ringing with authority. The villagers, witnessing the spectacle, rallied behind her, emboldened by her courage. The bandits, realizing they were outmatched, turned to flee, abandoning their spoils.

As the dust settled and the villagers cheered, Elinora basked in their admiration, her heart swelling with pride. "I can protect them!" she thought. But as the night wore on, she began to notice the elixir's effects fading, the exhilarating strength turning to exhaustion.

Realizing her powers were fleeting, she hurried home, aware that dawn would bring the end of her extraordinary day. As the first light of morning broke, she felt the last remnants of the potion dissipate. The power that had once surged through her faded away, leaving her breathless and weary.

But as she collapsed onto her bed, Elinora felt a strange sense of fulfillment. While the elixir had granted her powers for a single day, the impact of her actions would linger. She had united the villagers, inspired courage in their hearts, and protected her home.

The sun rose higher in the sky, casting a warm glow over Eldergrove. Elinora awoke, determined to carry forward the spirit of that extraordinary night. Though she had lost the elixir's powers, she realized that true strength came not from magic but from the bonds forged in adversity and the courage to stand up for what was right.

Days turned into weeks, and as Elinora continued her work in the apothecary, she inspired others to take action in their own lives. The villagers began to look out for one another, forming a tighter community. They learned that heroism lay not in the extraordinary but in the everyday choices to support and uplift each other.

In the end, the lesson of the Elixir of Ambrosia resonated deeply: power is fleeting, but the strength of community and the courage to act in the face of darkness is eternal. Elinora may have been just an ordinary herbalist, but she had sparked a flame of unity that would shine brightly in the hearts of the villagers, illuminating the path forward long after the magical storm had passed.

The Dreamweaver's Realm

In the quiet town of Reverie, where the line between dreams and reality blurred, an old legend whispered among the townsfolk. They spoke of a realm known as Nocturne, a place where dreams were spun like silk and intertwined with the waking world. It was said that those who ventured into Nocturne could reshape their destinies, but they risked losing themselves to the dreamscape if they were not careful.

Amelia, a restless artist, often found herself trapped in a cycle of unfulfilled aspirations. Each night, she would pour her heart into her paintings, only to wake up to blank canvases. Frustration gnawed at her spirit, and she yearned for a way to break free from the mundane chains of her life. One fateful evening, after another restless night, she stumbled upon a dusty old book in the town's forgotten library. The title read *The Secrets of Nocturne*, its pages filled with enchanting illustrations and tales of dreamweavers who could manipulate the fabric of dreams.

Intrigued, Amelia read about a ritual that could summon the dreamweavers and open a portal to Nocturne. Her heart raced with excitement and trepidation. "What do I have to lose?" she thought. That night, she gathered the ingredients: lavender for calm, moonstone for clarity, and a drop of her own blood to signify her intent. Under the light of a full moon, she performed the ritual, her voice steady as she chanted the incantation.

The air shimmered, and a portal of swirling mist opened before her. Taking a deep breath, she stepped through, feeling a rush of energy as reality melted away. She found herself standing in a vibrant landscape, where the sky danced in shades of indigo and emerald, and the air was filled with the scent of blooming dreams.

"Welcome, seeker of dreams," a melodic voice chimed. Turning, Amelia beheld a figure draped in flowing robes adorned with stars—a dreamweaver named Lysandra. "You have entered Nocturne. What do you desire?"

"I want to create art that inspires and connects with others," Amelia declared, her heart pounding with hope. "I want to turn my dreams into reality."

Lysandra smiled, her eyes twinkling like distant galaxies. "In Nocturne, you can shape your reality. But remember, every creation comes with a cost. Are you prepared to face your fears?"

With a nod, Amelia followed Lysandra deeper into Nocturne, where dreams were spun into existence. They passed through fields of color, where artists painted the sky with their imagination, and musicians wove melodies that resonated with the stars. Amelia's heart swelled with inspiration, and she felt an exhilarating sense of possibility.

Lysandra led her to a magnificent canvas that shimmered with liquid light. "Here, you can paint your dreams," she said, gesturing to the canvas. "But first, you must confront the shadows that lurk within you."

As Amelia approached the canvas, dark tendrils emerged, forming shapes that mirrored her insecurities—doubt, fear of failure, and the haunting voice of self-criticism. The shadows twisted around her, whispering their taunts, and for a moment, she felt the weight of their despair.

"Face them!" Lysandra urged, her voice steady. "These shadows are not your reality; they are merely reflections of your fears. You must reclaim your power!"

With determination, Amelia closed her eyes and breathed deeply. She visualized her dreams—the vibrant colors, the joyous laughter of those who connected with her art, the sense of fulfillment that came from sharing her soul. As she opened her eyes, she felt a surge of energy. She picked up a brush and dipped it into the canvas, allowing her emotions to flow freely.

With each stroke, the shadows began to dissipate, replaced by radiant colors that shimmered with hope and passion. The canvas came alive, revealing a breathtaking landscape filled with fantastical creatures, vibrant flowers, and luminous skies. Amelia poured her heart into the painting, and the more she embraced her dreams, the more the shadows faded into nothingness.

As she completed her masterpiece, the canvas shimmered with light, and Lysandra stepped forward, her expression proud. "You have conquered your fears and embraced your true self. Now, step back and witness the magic you've created."

Amelia stepped aside, her heart racing as the canvas glowed brightly. To her astonishment, the painting began to ripple and shift, transforming into a portal that beckoned her to enter. "What is this?" she gasped.

"This is your creation—a gateway to your dreams," Lysandra explained. "You can choose to step through and embrace the life you envision, but know this: once you leave, you cannot return to Nocturne."

Amelia stood at the threshold, her heart pounding with uncertainty. "What if I fail in the real world?"

"Then you will learn and grow, just as you have here," Lysandra replied gently. "True growth comes from embracing both success and failure."

With a deep breath, Amelia stepped through the portal, feeling a rush of energy as she crossed the threshold. She emerged back in her studio, the sunlight streaming through the window, illuminating her canvases. But now, she saw them with new eyes.

Instead of blank slates, they were filled with potential. Inspired by her experience in Nocturne, she began to paint with fervor, channeling her emotions into vibrant works of art that resonated with everyone who beheld them. As her art gained recognition, she found a community of fellow creatives who celebrated her journey.

Months later, as she reflected on her path, Amelia understood the profound lesson Nocturne had imparted: the journey to realizing one's dreams is as important as the dreams themselves. Embracing her fears had allowed her to create not just art, but connections and a life rich with purpose.

In the end, Amelia learned that while dreams can guide us, it is our willingness to confront our shadows and embrace the uncertainty of life that truly shapes our reality. Nocturne had gifted her not just a moment of inspiration, but the courage to become the artist she was always meant to be.

The Curse of the Jewel

In the bustling city of Valoria, where the streets teemed with merchants and the air was thick with the scent of spices, an ancient tale echoed through the alleys. It spoke of a cursed jewel known as the Heart of Nyx, a mesmerizing sapphire that shimmered with a deep, haunting light. Legends warned that whoever possessed the jewel would be granted immense wealth but would also face a string of misfortunes that would haunt them until their death.

Despite the warnings, the allure of the jewel proved irresistible to many, leading countless treasure hunters to their doom. But its last known location had been lost to time—until a young thief named Aric stumbled upon a tattered map in a forgotten corner of the city's archives. The map promised to lead to the Heart of Nyx, buried deep within the Whispering Woods, a place shrouded in mystery and danger.

Driven by dreams of fortune, Aric set out on his quest. A street-smart orphan with a knack for finding trouble, he had spent his life dodging the law and perfecting his skills in stealth. The thought of the jewel ignited a fire within him, a chance to escape the chains of poverty and create a new life. "Just one heist," he told himself, clutching the map tightly. "What could go wrong?"

After days of travel, Aric reached the Whispering Woods, where the trees loomed like ancient sentinels. The atmosphere was thick with an eerie stillness, the only sounds the rustle of leaves and the occasional distant hoot of an owl. As he ventured deeper, he felt a sense of foreboding, but he pressed on, determined to uncover the jewel's secrets.

After hours of navigating the twisted paths, Aric finally arrived at a clearing bathed in moonlight. At its center stood a stone pedestal, and atop it gleamed the Heart of Nyx, pulsating with an otherworldly glow. Aric's heart raced as he approached, the beauty of the jewel captivating him. "This is it!" he whispered, reaching out to take it.

As his fingers brushed the cool surface, a shiver ran down his spine. A low voice echoed around him. "You dare disturb my slumber?" Aric spun around, eyes wide with fear. From the shadows emerged a ghostly figure, a woman draped in tattered robes, her expression a mix of sorrow and anger.

"Who are you?" Aric stammered, stepping back.

"I am Selene, guardian of the Heart of Nyx," she replied, her voice ethereal. "Many have sought this jewel, drawn by its beauty and the promise of wealth. But it is a curse, not a gift. Those who possess it are doomed to suffer."

Aric hesitated, the weight of her words settling into his mind. "But I need this! I can't go back to my old life."

"Every wish comes at a price," Selene warned. "Take it, and you will gain riches, but you will lose what is most precious to you."

Ignoring her caution, Aric snatched the jewel from the pedestal, the moment of triumph quickly overshadowed by a wave of darkness. Instantly, the forest erupted in chaos. Shadows twisted and writhed, clawing at his heels as he fled, the jewel clutched tightly in his hands.

Days turned into weeks, and Aric returned to Valoria, basking in the riches the jewel had provided. But as the days passed, misfortune followed him like a shadow. His newfound wealth attracted thieves, and he was betrayed by those he had trusted. Ill fortune struck at every turn—his home was robbed, his friends turned against him, and illness crept into his life.

Haunted by the consequences of his greed, Aric sought out Selene once more, desperate for answers. "Please, help me! I didn't believe you. I thought I could handle it."

Selene appeared before him, her form shimmering with the light of the moon. "You have awakened the curse, Aric. To break it, you must return the Heart of Nyx to its rightful place and offer a sacrifice."

"A sacrifice?" he echoed, dread pooling in his stomach. "What kind of sacrifice?"

"Something you hold dear," she replied, her voice tinged with sadness. "Only then can the curse be lifted."

With a heavy heart, Aric pondered what he could give up. He looked at the riches surrounding him—gold coins, jewels, and fine silks. But as he gazed upon them, he realized they were meaningless without the connections he had lost. His heart ached for the friendships he had sacrificed in pursuit of wealth.

Finally, Aric made his decision. He returned to the Whispering Woods, the Heart of Nyx clutched tightly in his hand. As he reached the pedestal, he knelt and placed the jewel back in its rightful place. "I give up my wealth for the chance to regain my life," he declared, his voice resolute.

As the jewel settled into the stone, a brilliant light engulfed the clearing, and Aric felt a weight lift from his shoulders. Selene appeared before him, her expression softening. "You have chosen wisely. The true cost of the jewel was never in gold but in the bonds we forge and the love we nurture."

With a final flash of light, the curse shattered, and Aric was left alone in the clearing, the echoes of the past fading into the wind. He returned to Valoria, not with treasures but with newfound wisdom. The lessons learned through his trials were worth more than gold—he understood the value of connection and the importance of sincerity.

Though life would still bring challenges, Aric was no longer driven by greed. He rebuilt his relationships, offered help to those in need, and created a community that thrived on trust and support. The Heart of Nyx remained a legend, but its true magic lay not in its power to grant wishes, but in the reminder that our choices shape our destinies.

In giving up everything for a fleeting moment of glory, Aric found that what truly mattered was the journey back to himself and the bonds he had once forsaken.

The Valley of Enchantment

Nestled beyond the towering peaks of the Misty Mountains lay a hidden valley known as Eldergrove Hollow, a place whispered about in tales but seldom seen by human eyes. This secret realm was home to mythical creatures—graceful unicorns, mischievous fairies, wise centaurs, and gentle dragons—who lived in harmony, untouched by the chaos of the outside world.

Liora, a weary traveler burdened by the weight of her mundane life, often felt drawn to the mountains in search of solace. A talented botanist, she sought the rare plants rumored to grow in the valley, believed to possess healing properties. Yet, beneath her scientific curiosity, a deeper yearning stirred—a longing for magic and wonder, for a connection to something greater than herself.

One fateful day, as Liora trekked through a forest on the mountain's edge, she stumbled upon a narrow, winding path. An inexplicable pull guided her feet, and she followed the trail, her heart racing with excitement. The air shimmered with magic, and the scent of blooming wildflowers filled her senses. After a short hike, she emerged into a sun-drenched meadow that felt alive with energy.

Before her stretched Eldergrove Hollow, a breathtaking landscape adorned with vibrant flora and shimmering streams. Creatures of all kinds frolicked in the fields, their laughter harmonizing with the gentle rustle of leaves. Liora gasped in wonder, her heart swelling with joy. She had found the mythical valley she had only dreamed of.

As she ventured deeper, she encountered a majestic unicorn grazing peacefully by a crystal-clear pond. Its coat gleamed in the sunlight, and its eyes held an ancient wisdom. "Welcome, traveler," the unicorn spoke, its voice melodious and soothing. "You have crossed into our realm. Few humans find their way here."

"I'm Liora," she replied, her voice barely above a whisper. "I seek rare plants for healing, but I never imagined I would find a place like this."

The unicorn regarded her thoughtfully. "Eldergrove Hollow thrives on harmony. The plants you seek are sacred, nourished by the magic of our home. If your intentions are pure, you may take what you need."

Grateful, Liora explored the valley, her heart racing as she discovered plants that glowed with otherworldly light. She gathered samples, her mind racing with ideas for their potential uses. Yet, as she collected, she felt a deeper connection forming between herself and the valley. The land felt like a part of her, and the creatures welcomed her as one of their own.

As the sun dipped below the horizon, casting golden hues across the landscape, Liora found herself in a clearing where a gathering was taking place. The fairies danced in a circle, their laughter echoing like chimes in the wind. The centaurs spoke of old tales, their voices rich with history, while dragons soared above, leaving trails of light in their wake.

"Join us, Liora!" called a fairy, her wings sparkling like the stars. "Celebrate with us tonight! You have brought a breath of fresh air to our valley."

Feeling a surge of joy, Liora joined the festivities. For the first time in years, she felt truly alive, embraced by the magic of Eldergrove Hollow. As night enveloped the valley, she danced under the stars, her worries fading away.

But as dawn approached, a shadow fell over her heart. Liora knew she would eventually have to leave this enchanting place and return to her ordinary life. The thought weighed heavily on her, and she felt a sense of loss creeping in.

Suddenly, a wise centaur approached her, sensing her turmoil. "You are troubled, Liora. This valley has awakened something within you. Do not let the world beyond dim your light."

"But I can't stay," she replied, her voice trembling. "I have responsibilities, a life to return to."

"True," the centaur said, his eyes deep and knowing. "But remember, you carry the magic of this place within you. You can share what you've learned and inspire others, bridging the gap between our worlds."

As the first rays of sunlight pierced through the trees, Liora felt a glimmer of hope. Perhaps she could take the essence of Eldergrove Hollow with her, spreading its magic in her own way. "I will," she vowed, her voice steady. "I'll share the wonders I've experienced here."

With the dawn came the time to depart. The creatures gathered to bid her farewell, each one offering a token of their appreciation—a flower from the unicorn, a tiny vial of fairy dust, and a feather from a dragon. These gifts would serve as reminders of the magic she had discovered.

As Liora crossed back through the path leading to the mountains, she felt the weight of her journey shift. She carried not just the physical tokens but a renewed sense of purpose and inspiration. The valley would always be a part of her, a source of strength in times of doubt.

When she returned to her village, Liora shared her knowledge of the plants and their healing properties, emphasizing the importance of living in harmony with nature. The villagers listened, captivated by her stories and the spark of magic she brought back with her.

In time, Liora became a beacon of hope, reminding her community of the beauty that existed beyond their mundane lives. The hidden valley and its mystical creatures lived on in the hearts of those who listened, a reminder that magic is not confined to distant lands; it resides within each of us, waiting to be awakened.

And in the depths of her soul, Liora knew that as long as she remembered Eldergrove Hollow, its magic would never truly fade. It taught her that life is a tapestry woven from dreams and realities, and it is our connection to both that creates the most beautiful of destinies.

The Secrets of Sylvan Grove

In the heart of the Kingdom of Eldoria, whispers spoke of an enchanted forest known as Sylvan Grove. The trees within the forest towered majestically, their leaves shimmering with an ethereal glow, and a mist of vibrant colors danced among the branches. It was said that Sylvan Grove held the secret to eternal youth, a promise that lured many into its depths. However, few returned, and those who did were forever changed.

Among the curious souls was Elowen, a spirited woman in her late thirties who had spent her life devoted to her work as a healer. Despite her skills and knowledge, she often felt the weight of time pressing down on her, each wrinkle a reminder of the years that had passed. As she prepared for another day in her modest cottage, she overheard the villagers discussing the legends of Sylvan Grove.

"The forest holds the Elixir of Eternity," a farmer proclaimed, his eyes wide with excitement. "If you can reach the Heart Tree, you'll be granted eternal youth!"

Elowen felt a surge of determination. Perhaps the elixir could help her not only regain her youth but also amplify her healing abilities, allowing her to help more people. After a restless night of contemplation, she decided to seek the enchanted forest.

Equipped with little more than her healing herbs and a sturdy walking stick, Elowen set off at dawn, her heart pounding with anticipation. As she entered the forest, the atmosphere shifted; the air was thick with magic, and the vibrant colors pulsed with life. Birds sang sweet melodies, and the gentle rustle of leaves felt like the whispers of old spirits.

After hours of wandering, Elowen encountered a peculiar creature—a small, luminescent fox with sparkling fur and wise, knowing eyes. "You seek the Heart Tree, do you not?" the fox asked, its voice soft and melodic.

"Yes," Elowen replied, her excitement palpable. "I want to find the Elixir of Eternity."

The fox tilted its head, its expression contemplative. "The elixir is not just a gift; it comes with a choice. Are you prepared for the consequences of immortality?"

Elowen hesitated, the weight of the fox's words sinking in. "I... I just want to help others. I've seen too much suffering."

"Very well," the fox said, its eyes sparkling. "Follow me, but remember: the forest will test your resolve. Only those with true intentions may reach the Heart Tree."

Elowen followed the fox deeper into Sylvan Grove, encountering trials that tested her heart and spirit. She faced illusions of her past—moments of loss, regret, and self-doubt. Each time she faltered, the forest seemed to shift, leading her further from her goal. But with each challenge, she found strength in her purpose. "I want to heal," she reminded herself, fighting against the illusions.

After what felt like days of wandering, Elowen finally stood before the Heart Tree, its immense trunk gnarled and ancient, branches reaching toward the sky like arms in prayer. At its base, a small pool glimmered with an otherworldly light, the Elixir of Eternity swirling within it.

"You have made it," the fox said, appearing at her side. "Now, you must choose. Will you drink the elixir and become immortal, or will you turn back, knowing that your life is a precious gift meant to be lived, not extended?"

Elowen knelt by the pool, her heart racing. The prospect of eternal youth was tantalizing, yet the weight of the decision pressed heavily on her. She thought of the people she had helped, the lives she had touched, and the fleeting moments that defined her journey.

"What good is eternal youth," she pondered aloud, "if I am destined to witness the world change around me while I remain unchanged?"

The fox regarded her with approval. "Wisdom lies in understanding that life's beauty is in its impermanence. Choose to embrace the gift of each moment, rather than chase the illusion of eternity."

With a newfound clarity, Elowen stood up and took a step back from the shimmering pool. "I will not drink the elixir. I choose to cherish the time I have and use my gifts to help others while I can."

As soon as she spoke those words, the Heart Tree glowed with a radiant light, and the elixir faded into a cascade of sparkling mist, enveloping her in warmth. The fox smiled, its form shimmering as it transformed into a spirit of the forest. "You have chosen wisely, Elowen. Your decision honors the cycle of life, and your healing powers will grow even stronger."

In an instant, Elowen found herself back at the forest's entrance, the sun shining brightly overhead. The villagers greeted her with surprise and joy, as if she had been gone only moments. Yet something inside her had changed. She felt lighter, more vibrant, and filled with purpose.

With the lessons of Sylvan Grove etched into her heart, Elowen devoted herself to her craft with renewed vigor. She shared her experiences, encouraging others to find beauty in their lives, regardless of age. Her reputation as a healer grew, not just for her skills, but for the wisdom she imparted.

In time, Elowen realized that true beauty lies not in the preservation of youth, but in the moments that shape us—the connections we forge, the love we share, and the compassion we offer. As she moved through the seasons of her life, she embraced each wrinkle and scar as a testament to her journey, a map of the life she had lived fully, fiercely, and with grace.

And so, in the end, the Heart Tree and its wisdom remained alive within her, reminding her that while life is transient, its magic resides in the choices we make and the love we give.

Threads of Destiny

In the quaint village of Eldenwood, nestled between rolling hills and sprawling meadows, there existed a small, curious shop known as "The Woven Whimsy." Run by a reclusive old woman named Agatha, the shop was filled with an array of fabrics, threads, and tapestries, each more vibrant than the last. However, the villagers often whispered about a particular tapestry that hung in the back room, draped in shadows and mystery—a magical tapestry said to depict the future.

Many were drawn to the shop, hoping to glimpse their fates woven into the intricate patterns. Yet Agatha had a strict rule: no one was permitted to view the tapestry without first understanding the weight of their desires. For to see one's future was a double-edged sword; it could grant hope or shatter dreams.

One crisp autumn day, a young woman named Elara entered the shop, her spirit heavy with uncertainty. She was at a crossroads in her life, grappling with the choice between pursuing her dreams of becoming a painter or adhering to the expectations of her family to take over the family bakery. The vivid colors and textures of Agatha's fabrics captivated her, but it was the whispers of the tapestry that called to her soul.

"Ah, I sense a seeker of truth," Agatha said, her voice as soothing as the warm breeze. "What burdens your heart, child?"

Elara hesitated, her heart racing. "I want to know my future. I want to see if my dreams as an artist can come true."

Agatha's wise eyes sparkled. "The tapestry can reveal glimpses of what is to come, but remember, it does not dictate your path. Your choices weave the fabric of your destiny."

"I understand," Elara replied, determination etched on her face. "I'm ready."

Agatha led Elara to the back room, where the tapestry hung like a guardian of secrets. Its colors swirled in mesmerizing patterns, shimmering in hues that seemed to shift with every glance. As Elara stood before it, she felt a surge of energy pulse through her.

"Touch it, and allow yourself to see," Agatha instructed gently.

With a trembling hand, Elara reached out and pressed her palm against the cool fabric. In an instant, images flooded her mind—visions of her future unfolding before her like a vivid dream. She saw herself standing in a bustling art gallery, her paintings displayed for all to admire. The warmth of applause filled her heart, and joy radiated from her being.

But then the images shifted. She saw herself struggling to make ends meet, surrounded by empty canvases and brushes coated in dust. Doubt crept into her mind, and she felt the weight of disappointment. Tears pricked her eyes as she glimpsed the potential pain of failure, the fear of letting her family down.

"Enough!" she gasped, pulling her hand away from the tapestry, heart racing. "I can't take this!"

Agatha placed a comforting hand on her shoulder. "The future is not set in stone. What you saw are possibilities based on your current path. Embrace your passion, and remember that every artist faces challenges."

Elara took a deep breath, trying to quell the turmoil within her. "But what if I choose wrong?"

"Choices shape our journey," Agatha replied, her voice steady. "You must trust yourself. The tapestry shows potential outcomes, but it cannot predict the strength of your resolve."

Determined to forge her own destiny, Elara left the shop, the images of the tapestry lingering in her mind. For the first time, she felt the weight of her dreams, both exhilarating and terrifying.

As days turned into weeks, she devoted herself to her art, pouring her heart into every stroke of the brush. Yet doubt still crept in, whispering fears of failure and insecurity. With each painting, she wondered if she was making the right choice, but she pushed through, inspired by the possibility she had glimpsed in the tapestry.

One evening, as she was working late in her studio, a knock at the door interrupted her thoughts. It was a local art dealer, intrigued by the whispers of her talent. He expressed interest in showcasing her work in an upcoming exhibit.

Elara's heart raced with excitement and disbelief. "You really want my paintings?"

"Absolutely," he replied, his eyes bright with enthusiasm. "Your art has a unique voice, and it deserves to be seen."

As she prepared for the exhibit, Elara found herself overwhelmed by fear and anticipation. Memories of the tapestry's visions swirled in her mind—her dreams of success mingled with the haunting specter of failure. On the night of the exhibit, she stood before the crowd, her heart pounding.

The gallery buzzed with energy, and as she unveiled her paintings, she felt a mix of hope and anxiety. Would they resonate with the audience? Would she be accepted?

As the evening unfolded, applause and compliments washed over her like a wave. Her paintings spoke to the hearts of those who beheld them, and for the first time, Elara felt a deep sense of belonging. The fears that had once clouded her heart began to fade, replaced by the joy of sharing her passion with the world.

After the exhibit, as she basked in the warmth of her success, Elara realized the true lesson of the tapestry: the future is not merely a prediction; it is a reflection of the choices we make and the courage we muster to pursue our passions.

When she returned to Agatha's shop to express her gratitude, the old woman smiled knowingly. "You have woven your own destiny, child. The tapestry showed you possibilities, but it was your heart that shaped the outcome."

With newfound clarity, Elara understood that the power of the tapestry lay not in its ability to reveal the future but in its capacity to inspire courage and self-belief. And as she stepped out into the world, she carried with her the knowledge that the fabric of her life was woven by her choices, one vibrant thread at a time.

The Warding of Willow Creek

In the secluded village of Willow Creek, surrounded by ancient forests and shimmering lakes, the night sky twinkled with stars, each one a whisper of magic. Among the village's inhabitants was a young witch named Lyra, a vibrant soul with a wild mane of dark hair and emerald-green eyes that sparkled with determination. She was the youngest member of a long line of witches who had guarded the village and its secrets for centuries, yet she struggled to master her powers.

Lyra had always felt the pull of magic within her, but it remained just out of reach, elusive like the morning mist. Every evening, she practiced spells in the quiet solitude of her room, pouring over old tomes filled with ancient wisdom. Her grandmother, the coven's matriarch, often warned her, "With great power comes great responsibility, my dear. Do not rush the journey; you must learn to harness your gifts with patience."

But impatience nagged at Lyra's heart. She yearned to be a protector like her grandmother and the witches before her. Rumors had begun to swirl around the village of a dark presence lurking in the woods, and the coven felt the growing unease in the air. Lyra was determined to prove herself worthy of her lineage, to protect her coven, and to uncover the source of the encroaching darkness.

One moonlit night, while the villagers slept soundly, Lyra crept into the forest, drawn by a strange energy that pulsed like a heartbeat. As she wandered deeper, she stumbled upon a hidden glade illuminated by silvery moonlight. In the center stood a magnificent ancient tree, its bark twisted and gnarled, with branches that reached for the stars. Lyra felt a magnetic pull toward it.

"The Tree of Whispers," she breathed, recognizing the legendary tree from the tales of her youth. It was said to hold the wisdom of the ages, a source of power for those pure of heart.

With a deep breath, Lyra approached the tree and placed her hand against its bark. Instantly, a rush of energy surged through her, filling her with warmth and clarity. "Teach me," she whispered, closing her eyes and surrendering to the magic of the moment.

Visions flooded her mind—images of her ancestors, the coven united against darkness, and the tree standing strong through the ages. But amidst the visions, a shadow flickered, a dark figure lurking just beyond the edges of her awareness. "Find the source," it seemed to whisper. "Protect what is yours."

Lyra opened her eyes, heart pounding. The forest felt alive with possibilities. Determined, she decided to return to the village to warn her fellow witches about the impending danger.

However, as she made her way back, she sensed a disturbance in the air. The shadows felt thicker, and a chill ran down her spine. Suddenly, she stumbled upon a clearing where the dark figure from her vision stood—a man cloaked in shadows, his eyes glowing with an unsettling light.

"Ah, the young witch," he sneered, his voice smooth and dangerous. "I've been waiting for you."

"Who are you?" Lyra demanded, her voice steady despite the fear that gripped her.

"I am Malachai, a sorcerer banished long ago by your coven. But now, I have returned to reclaim what was taken from me." His eyes narrowed as he pointed a finger toward the village. "Your precious tree, your magic. It will all belong to me!"

Fear mixed with anger surged within Lyra. She remembered the Tree of Whispers and the power it held. "You won't harm my coven," she declared, her voice stronger now. "I will protect them."

Malachai laughed, a sound that echoed through the clearing. "You think you can stop me? You're just a girl who hasn't yet learned to wield her powers."

But as his laughter faded, Lyra felt a surge of determination. She recalled the wisdom of the tree, the strength of her ancestors, and the bond of her coven. Drawing on the energy that coursed through her, she raised her hands and summoned a protective barrier of light.

The light shimmered like a beacon, pushing back the shadows that threatened to envelop her. Malachai's expression shifted from amusement to shock as he was forced back, struggling against the force of her magic. "What is this?"

"It's the strength of unity," Lyra replied, her heart pounding with newfound confidence. "You underestimate the power of our coven."

With a surge of energy, she called forth the spirits of her ancestors, feeling their presence around her. The light intensified, wrapping around Malachai like a vine, binding him in place. "You will not harm my home!"

With one final incantation, she unleashed a wave of energy that sent Malachai fleeing into the depths of the forest, his dark form vanishing into the night. The shadows lifted, and the air felt lighter, filled with the fragrance of wildflowers and the warmth of the moonlight.

Breathless and exhilarated, Lyra returned to her village, where the coven awaited her. As she shared her tale, she felt the warmth of their acceptance and pride. She had faced her fears and proven her strength.

From that day on, Lyra continued to learn and grow, embracing her powers with newfound confidence. She understood that the journey to mastery would take time, but the love and support of her coven would guide her. And as she stood before the Tree of Whispers, she knew that she would always carry the light of unity within her heart.

In the end, Lyra learned that true power comes not from the magic one wields, but from the connections forged through love, courage, and the willingness to stand up for what is right. As the moon shone brightly over Willow Creek, she knew that she was not just a young witch; she was a guardian of hope, ready to protect her home and all who dwelled within it.

The Gilded Shadows

In a land where the sun set ablaze the skies with golden hues, tales of a fabled city of gold known as Eldoria had long captivated the hearts of adventurers and dreamers alike. Nestled deep within the uncharted reaches of the Echoing Mountains, the city was said to be guarded by mythical beasts—creatures of both wonder and terror that would protect its riches from those deemed unworthy.

Among the seekers of fortune was a seasoned explorer named Rowan, a man with a reputation for boldness and an insatiable thirst for discovery. With tousled hair, sun-kissed skin, and a weathered map clutched in his hand, he embarked on his greatest adventure yet. Whispers of Eldoria echoed in his mind, fueling his ambition as he ventured forth from the coastal town of Beren's Hollow.

Rowan's journey began in a bustling market, where rumors fluttered like the banners overhead. "To find Eldoria, you must first conquer the beasts that guard its gates," warned an old woman selling trinkets. "Many have tried, but few have returned."

"I'll be the one to return with tales of glory," Rowan declared, his heart racing at the thought of riches and fame. He spent his last coins on supplies—provisions, a sturdy rope, and a talisman said to grant protection against the creatures of the wild.

After days of travel, Rowan reached the foot of the Echoing Mountains, where the air was thick with mist and mystery. The path wound upward, cloaked in shadow, and as he climbed, he felt the weight of unseen eyes upon him. Each step resonated with the heartbeat of the mountains, an echo of ancient power.

As dusk fell, the forest around him grew eerily silent. Suddenly, a low growl reverberated through the trees. Rowan froze, scanning the darkness until a massive shape emerged—an enormous feline creature with golden fur and eyes like molten amber. It was a Gilded Panther, one of the legendary guardians of Eldoria.

"Turn back, seeker," the panther spoke, its voice deep and rumbling. "You are not worthy of the treasures that lie within."

Rowan's heart raced, but his resolve hardened. "I seek not only gold but knowledge and adventure. I will not turn back without a fight."

The panther's eyes narrowed. "You will face trials beyond your understanding. If you wish to proceed, you must first prove your worth."

With a flick of its tail, the panther disappeared into the shadows, leaving Rowan to ponder the challenge before him. Moments later, a shimmering portal opened before him, and he stepped through, entering a grand arena filled with vibrant flora and ethereal light.

In the center stood the panther, flanked by other mythical beasts—a majestic griffon, a sly fox with wings, and a towering stone golem. "You will face each of us in turn," the panther announced. "Only by proving your heart is pure can you access the lost city."

Rowan nodded, adrenaline coursing through his veins as he prepared for the first trial. The griffon swooped down, talons gleaming as it challenged him to a race across the arena. With quick reflexes, Rowan leaped into action, sprinting toward the finish line. As he ran, he found himself caught in a whirlwind of wind and feathers, the griffon pushing him to his limits. In a moment of ingenuity, he leaped onto a nearby branch, swinging himself to victory.

Impressed by his skill and determination, the griffon stepped aside, allowing Rowan to face the next beast. The winged fox darted around him, weaving through the trees, challenging him to a game of wits. "Solve my riddle, and you may pass. Fail, and you shall remain here forever."

With a flick of its tail, the fox posed a riddle that twisted his mind. After deep contemplation, Rowan cracked the code, realizing the answer was rooted in unity. "The answer is 'together,'" he declared, and the fox nodded, granting him passage.

As Rowan approached the final trial, he faced the stone golem, a massive creature carved from ancient rock. "To pass, you must face your greatest fear," it rumbled, its voice echoing through the arena.

Rowan felt a chill run down his spine as visions of failure flooded his mind—losing everything he had worked for, being trapped in mediocrity. But he steadied himself, remembering the thrill of adventure and the people who believed in him. "I fear not failure but the regret of not trying!" he shouted, and the golem, recognizing his courage, stepped aside.

Having completed the trials, the beasts led Rowan to the entrance of Eldoria, a grand archway adorned with intricate carvings of ancient lore. As he crossed the threshold, he was met with a breathtaking sight—a city of shimmering gold, where sunlight danced off every surface, and laughter filled the air.

However, as Rowan explored, he discovered something unexpected. The wealth of Eldoria was not measured solely in gold and riches; it was in the community, the vibrant lives of its inhabitants who thrived together, sharing their knowledge, stories, and dreams.

"Welcome, seeker," a wise elder greeted him. "You have proven your worth, but remember, true treasure lies not in gold but in the bonds we forge and the legacy we leave behind."

As Rowan spent time in Eldoria, he learned that the greatest adventures were not merely about wealth but about connection, purpose, and the pursuit of dreams. When it was time to leave, he carried with him not just the glimmer of gold but the wisdom of community.

As he descended the mountains back to Willow Creek, Rowan realized that the journey to Eldoria had transformed him. He understood that while the allure of riches was powerful, the true essence of adventure lay in the connections forged along the way.

And so, he returned home, ready to share his stories and create a legacy that would inspire others to seek their own paths, to embrace challenges, and to treasure the bonds that would lead them to their own hidden cities of gold.

The Guardian of Aetheria

In the craggy peaks of the Eldar Mountains, where the winds howled like lost souls and the air shimmered with magic, an ancient dragon named Kaelthar perched atop a rocky outcropping. His scales glinted like polished emeralds in the sunlight, and his amber eyes held centuries of wisdom. Kaelthar was the last of his kind, a noble guardian tasked with protecting the portal to Aetheria, a realm said to be filled with wonders and dangers untold.

For ages, the portal had remained hidden from the eyes of humankind, concealed behind a veil of illusion. Only those who were truly worthy could find their way to it. Over the years, many had sought the legendary realm, driven by dreams of power and glory, but none had succeeded. Each time, Kaelthar had turned them away, their greed revealing their unworthiness.

One fateful day, a young woman named Seraphine scaled the treacherous cliffs of the Eldar Mountains, driven by a burning desire to uncover the truth of her past. Orphaned at a young age, she had been raised in a small village, where the stories of dragons and hidden realms had sparked her imagination. She felt a connection to something greater, an urge to discover who she was meant to be.

As she reached the summit, the winds whipped around her, and the majestic figure of Kaelthar emerged from the mist. "What brings you to my mountain, child?" he rumbled, his voice deep and resonant.

"I seek the portal to Aetheria," Seraphine replied, her heart pounding with a mix of fear and excitement. "I must know my destiny."

Kaelthar studied her intently, his gaze piercing through her facade. "Many have come before you, driven by ambition and greed. What makes you different?"

Seraphine took a deep breath, drawing upon her resolve. "I don't seek power. I want to find my family and understand where I come from. I've always felt lost, and I believe Aetheria holds the answers."

The dragon considered her words, the winds howling in response. "Your intentions are noble, but to reach Aetheria, you must pass a trial. Only those with a pure heart can open the portal."

"I'm ready," she declared, determination shining in her eyes.

With a nod, Kaelthar unfurled his massive wings, and the ground trembled beneath him. "Very well. You must face the Trial of Truth. Follow me."

Seraphine watched as the dragon soared into the sky, leaving a trail of shimmering scales. She followed, her heart racing as they descended into a hidden valley shrouded in mist. In the center stood a massive stone circle, ancient runes etched into the ground.

"Step into the circle," Kaelthar instructed, hovering above her. "You will be shown visions of your past. Face them, and let the truth guide you."

Taking a deep breath, Seraphine stepped into the circle. The air crackled with energy, and suddenly, she was engulfed in swirling colors. Visions flooded her mind—images of a warm home, laughter, and the faces of her parents, but then they twisted into scenes of sorrow. She saw the fire that had consumed her childhood home, the chaos, the screams, and the emptiness that followed.

"No!" she cried, the pain of loss clawing at her heart. "I didn't want to see this!"

The visions shifted again, showing her moments of resilience—her determination to survive, her quest for knowledge, and the friendships she had forged along the way. A glimmer of hope sparked within her. "This is who I am," she realized. "I am more than my past."

As the visions faded, she stood trembling in the circle, her heart pounding. Kaelthar landed beside her, his expression inscrutable. "What did you learn?"

"I learned that my past does not define me," Seraphine replied, her voice steadying. "I can shape my own future."

"Wise words for one so young," Kaelthar replied, a hint of approval in his tone. "You have faced your truth, and now you may access the portal."

With a wave of his claw, the runes glowed brightly, and a shimmering gateway appeared before them. Seraphine stepped forward, the air humming with magic. She turned to Kaelthar, gratitude shining in her eyes. "Thank you for believing in me."

"Remember, child," he said, his voice resonating with depth. "Aetheria will show you wonders, but it is you who must choose what to take from it. The journey is just as important as the destination."

With that, Seraphine stepped through the portal, her heart racing with anticipation. Aetheria unfolded before her—a breathtaking realm filled with vibrant colors, floating islands, and creatures beyond imagination. Yet, as she explored, she realized that the answers she sought were not just about finding her family, but about discovering her true self.

In Aetheria, she encountered beings of light who shared their wisdom and challenges. They taught her that every choice shapes destiny and that the heart's desires must be tempered with understanding. With each lesson learned, Seraphine grew stronger and more confident, embracing her identity as an explorer of not just realms, but of her own spirit.

Eventually, after what felt like an eternity of growth and adventure, Seraphine returned to the portal that led back to Willow Creek. As she stepped back into the familiar terrain, she felt an unshakeable sense of belonging.

Kaelthar awaited her, a knowing smile on his face. "Welcome back, seeker. What have you found?"

"I found my strength," Seraphine said, her voice firm. "I learned that my past is a part of me, but it does not control my future. I am ready to forge my own path."

Kaelthar nodded, pride glimmering in his eyes. "Then go forth, brave one. Share your story, inspire others, and remember that the journey is ongoing. You hold the key to your destiny."

As Seraphine left the mountains, she understood that true power lies not just in the pursuit of dreams but in the wisdom gathered along the way. The lessons from Aetheria would guide her as she crafted a life full of purpose and passion, forever intertwined with the magic of her adventures.

Get Another Book Free

We love writing and have produced many books.

As a thank you for being one of our amazing readers, we'd like to offer you a free book.

To claim this limited-time offer, visit the site below and enter your name and email address.

You'll receive one of our great books directly to your email, completely free!

https://free.copypeople.com

Also by Morgan B. Blake

The Hidden Truth
Silent Obsession

Standalone
Temporal Havoc
The AI Resurrection
99942 Apophis
The Shadows We Keep
Whispers of the Forgotten
Christmas Chronicles: Enchanted Stories for the Holiday Season
Realm of Enchantment Tales from the Mystic Lands